24109

D0053863

Nicki

by
Ann Howard Creel

★ American Girl™

For Jessica and Kelly and all dog lovers everywhere

Published by Pleasant Company Publications
Copyright © 2007 by American Girl, LLC
Printed in China
07 08 09 10 11 LEO 10 9 8 7 6 5 4 3 2 1
Illustrations by Doron Ben-Ami

Questions or comments? Call 1-800-845-0005, visit our Web site at **americangirl.com**, or write to Customer Service, American Girl, 8400 Fairway Place, Middleton, WI 53562-0497.

The characters and events portrayed in this book are fictitious. Any similarity to real persons, living or dead, is coincidental and not intended by the author.

The following individuals and organizations have generously given permission to reprint photos contained in "True Story": pp. 122–23—photo courtesy of Sandra Barker; p. 122—photos by Karyl Carmignani, used with permission of Canine Companions for Independence (CCI); pp. 124–26—courtesy of Sandra Barker; p. 127—photos used with permission of CCI, Freedom Service Dogs, and Wisconsin Academy of Graduate Service Dogs (WAGS); p. 128—photo by Chris Kittredge, courtesy of CCI; p. 130—photo by Becky Skrudland

Assistance-Dog Etiquette used with the permission of Wisconsin Academy of Graduate Service Dogs (WAGS).

Cataloguing-in-Publication Data available from the Library of Congress.

24109

Contents

1

One Little Word

Everyone needs help.

And when people ask me for it, I like to give it if I can. I'm really a very helpful girl. But I have this problem: Even if I can't help, I just can't seem to make that sound, you know the one—when you put your tongue on the roof of your mouth behind your teeth and then open your lips like a circle and say, "No."

That's my big problem: I'm ten years old, but I haven't learned how to say that one little word.

The day started like all the others. It was a morning in the middle of April, and my father asked me to muck out the horse stables, which is a nice way of saying that you clean out all the horse droppings, which are more like bombs, and then put down fresh straw in the stalls. I was running late for school, but I said, "Okay."

Back inside, my little brother, Adam, asked me to check the last of his math homework problems, the ones I'd helped him get started on the night before, and I said, "Sure."

Mom asked me to help with the breakfast dishes and then to pack school lunches for Adam and me, and I did manage a very long *sighhh* . . . before I did it.

Then she said, "Nicki, I have something to tell you." It was Mom's serious voice.

I finished cutting the sandwiches in half and put them in plastic wrap. That's when I noticed that Mom had stopped working and was sitting down at the kitchen table rubbing the back of her neck.

This was really serious.

"Okay," I said and tried not to look at the clock. Thirteen minutes before the school bus would arrive at the end of the road that leads to our ranch. Adam and I are the first kids to be picked up in the morning and the last to be dropped off in the afternoon. We're the end of the line. It's just Adam and me, a few rusty mailboxes, and the occasional prairie dog.

Mom said, "I have some . . . interesting news."

Interesting? I thought to myself. "What?" I said to Mom.

"You know the little brother or sister we're expecting this fall?" Mom touched her belly, which had just begun to stretch out her khakis and sweater. "Well, it's going to be two instead of just one."

"Two?" I tried not to gasp. "You mean *twins?*"

"Yes," answered Mom. "I found out yesterday at the doctor's office. I don't know if they're boys or girls, and I'm not sure that I want to know, but there are definitely *two* babies in here."

Twins? "Could it be one of each?" I asked.

"No. That's the one thing we know for sure. They're identical."

I couldn't quite get my mind around twins. Instead I stared out the window over the kitchen sink. Dad was out there as usual, checking on the pigs in our big, heated "pig parlor." Thank goodness he hadn't asked me to do anything with the pigs this morning! You have to be careful not to get the smell of pig on your clothes, because it doesn't go away. I like the pigs okay, but they have this certain odor, and I don't exactly want all the new kids at school to know that we raise *swine.* We also stable horses for people from Denver and graze some cattle, but pork is our main thing. You know, for bacon, sausage, chops, and ham. We even sell the manure for fertilizer—that's the *wurst* of it.

I turned to Mom. "Is everything okay? With the twins, I mean?"

She brightened. "Perfect. No problems. I'm just going to have to take it easy around here."

Easy? *Easy* is not a word that fits around here at Twilight Ranch. Our place has such a peaceful name, but there's always work to do. Sometimes I wish I lived in a regular house with a small yard, like some of the homes in town. Kids who live there don't have so many chores to do.

Dad came in to refill his Thermos with hot coffee. He was wearing his usual jeans and plaid shirt under a work jacket.

"Did you hear our good news?" he said to me, and I nodded. "Two for the price of one." He didn't even unzip his jacket, and his work boots were leaving big fudgy mud clods on the kitchen floor. I knew I'd be the one to sweep those up later. "Now we have to pick two girls' names and two boys' names instead of just one of each," he said.

Mom said, "Two names. Two cribs. Double the diapers."

"But think about it: how many people have twins in their families?" Dad said with a grin.

"Exactly," replied Mom. "We're lucky."

Is she trying to convince herself or me? I wondered. I remembered the tiny identical faces in double strollers

I'd seen at the mall in Denver. And there's a pair of twins in Adam's second-grade class, two redheaded pixies. I didn't say it, but I hoped the twins would be girls. That would be special. Two little sisters. Not that Adam wasn't a great kid, but I'd love to have sisters. I smiled for the first time that morning.

Dad went back outdoors, and Mom looked at me. "I have a favor to ask of you," she said. She glanced toward the old back porch Dad had already closed in for a nursery, and I followed her gaze. "Now I have to get the nursery ready for two instead of one, and the doctor told me not to take on any new projects." She had worry in her eyes. "The problem is that I made a commitment to train that service dog I told you about. Like the service dogs I trained before you and Adam were born? It's a great deal of fun, but it also involves a lot of time and responsibility."

I had liked the idea of watching my mom train a service dog and then, of course, of having a puppy around, but now . . . "Can't you back out?" I asked, glancing at the clock again. Ten minutes until the bus came.

Then my eyes traveled back to the window, beyond the pig parlor, to the nearby mountaintops, where new snow had recently fallen, and I tuned out.

All I could do was think about skiing again before spring really arrived. To me, skiing is like flying, like riding a couple of long narrow wings on my feet, only going down instead of up, all the way to where the mountains begin.

"I guess I could back out," Mom was saying when I tuned back in. "But service dogs end up helping people who have physical challenges, those in wheel-chairs, for example, and it's important work. I've told you some of the stories before. Remember the young lady who was able to do her own shopping for the first time because of her dog?"

I nodded and finished packing the lunch bags with fruit cups and chips for Adam and me.

"Dogs can be trained to help people with hearing losses, too. There are even *kids* who get service dogs—kids with Down syndrome or cerebral palsy, for example. I hate to back out." Then Mom said in a lower voice, "So I was hoping you would help me. You're so good with animals, Nicki. You'd be a natural."

"Me?" I spun around. "I don't know anything about training a service dog."

"I can still be the main handler. I just need a little extra help, that's all. There's a very experienced handler nearby in Denver who can advise us, too. I think you'd

"Me?" said Nicki. "I don't know anything about training a service dog."

enjoy it, Nicki. I really do. And think of the help you'd be providing to someone who needs it."

I had to admit I liked that idea. But I couldn't help thinking of my 4-H project from last year. I raised a lamb and got kind of sentimental about him, like a pet. I took first place at the county fair in the lamb showing, but then I had to give him up. I couldn't even hang up the blue ribbon in my room—it made me too sad, even though I'm a ranch girl who's supposed to understand such things.

"But Mom, when you train a dog, you come to like it, and then you have to give it away, right?"

She hesitated. "That's right. That's the whole idea. The dog goes on to work for someone and makes his or her life easier."

Okay, so *that* was pretty cool, and being a part of it would be fun. Ever since Mom had told me that she was going to train a service dog, I'd been looking forward to having a cute puppy around and watching what Mom did. The whole idea of helping someone really appealed to me, too, but now that she was asking me . . . I just kept thinking about that lamb. Look what had happened. I had ended up sad.

Adam clumped into the kitchen. My little brother has a thick patch of brown hair on top of his head that's always getting tangled up, just like he does when it comes to math. And he has so many freckles, they almost blend together. Adam's shoelaces are always untied and getting tangled, too.

He grabbed his lunch and said to me, "Let's go."

The clock again. Eight minutes left. Just enough time to race down the long road to meet the bus.

Mom was studying me and waiting for an answer. "So, what do you say?"

Playing dumb might work. "About what?"

"About helping me train the service dog."

Mom wasn't going to let this go. I could see in her eyes that she really wanted me to help her. But I had too many things to do as it was, and I didn't want to love and lose another animal. I wanted to say "Yes," but at the same time, inside my brain, I was shaking my head from one side to the other. *No, no, no.*

Mom said, "I have to let the service-dog people know today."

Adam was at the front door by then, holding it open. I felt the cold morning air rushing in.

He yelled, "We're going to miss the bus!"

Mom said, "The driver won't leave without you, Adam." Then she looked at me again. "Just a little help with the training. What do you say?"

I threw on my coat and grabbed my things for school. Then I tried to make that sound. I even put my tongue on the roof of my mouth and tried to make a circle with my lips.

Adam yelled again. "Nicki! Come on!"

I looked at Mom again. Twins? She already did so much in the house and on the ranch, in addition to doing home decorating for people with new homes or those in the midst of renovations. She depended on me. Adam depended on me. Everyone counted on me to be the reliable one. To help out.

My brain was still trying to shake my head from side to side. *No, no, no. I can't do this. I can't take on one more thing, and I don't want to get sad about it in the end, either. This is a bad idea.*

Mom was waiting. Adam was waiting. What would happen if I actually said "No"?

Well, I had zero time to find out. Or maybe I didn't want to find out.

"Okay," I finally said.

2

Moguls

Adam and I had to sprint down the road, careful
not to fall in the ruts made by my father's pickup truck.
My breath formed a sparkly fog I kept running through.
Around us the pastures were filled with gold grasses
spiking up through patches of old snow that were
beginning to steam in the sunlight. Above it all, my
mountains with all of their fresh, new snow leaned in.

Just as Mom had predicted, our bus driver was
waiting for us and opened the bus door with a *whoosh*.
"Morning," said Mrs. Christiansen.

I mumbled back, "Hi." Inside, Adam and I could
sit anywhere we wanted. Adam took his usual seat,
and I waited for Becca in the seat behind him.

Becca got on at the next stop. She sat down next
to me and said, "Hey."

I said, "Hey, you." It was our usual way to start
the morning.

Becca has been my best friend ever since we
started school. Her family does pretty much the same
things we do, but instead of pigs their main business is
chickens, which is almost as bad. Almost.

"Did you see the fresh snow up there?" she asked and pointed toward the slopes.

I smiled again. "Powder."

"But I heard on the news that they're closing some of the runs already. We have to go this weekend before it's too late." Becca gathered her thick red hair into a ponytail and then adjusted the funky black glasses that Mom and I had helped her pick out at the mall in Denver. "Okay? You're in?"

I looked at the mountains again. They looked like shiny white teeth biting into the blue, blue sky. I couldn't wait to get back up there. It had already been three weeks since I'd last gone skiing.

"What's wrong?" asked Becca.

I shrugged. "My mom is going to have twins."

"Wow. Twins?"

"I know. How cool is that?"

"So, what's the problem?" Becca asked, tilting her head.

"She has to take it easier. I'll have to help her out even more."

Becca sighed. "She'll understand. We *have* to go. It's probably the last good weekend of the season."

"I'll ask," I said.

"My mom will drive us up there and ski, too.

Remember, we can get cheap lift tickets now that she's on ski patrol." Becca's mom is a weird combination of ranch mother and fitness fanatic. She even jogs on the dirt roads that run between ranches.

"Saturday morning," Becca said. "First thing."

By the time we arrived at school, the bus was full of other kids who live on ranches and small farms outside our small town. The bus pulled up in back of a line of nice cars and SUVs owned by the parents of kids who'd moved in recently. Escaping city life or something like that, they live in big log-and-glass houses that perch on the sides of the slopes and never have to worry about the smell of pig. Some of those kids even have their own cell phones and wear a different pair of shoes or boots every day of the week.

School started out like any other school day, too. Mrs. Baxter, my fourth-grade teacher, is my favorite teacher of all time. Of course, every year, my new teacher is my favorite of all time. But Mrs. Baxter is special. She's young and blue-eyed and just had a baby boy. She can draw anything on the whiteboard, and she always decorates our classroom from floor to ceiling in different themes, depending on the season. Lately she had been getting the room ready for spring.

After spelling and before lunchtime, she came by my desk. "Would you stay behind for a minute, Nicki? I have something to ask you."

I said, "Sure." Like always.

I finished my spelling homework during our free time, and when all the other kids filed out for lunch, I went up to Mrs. Baxter's desk.

She said, "You know the gala we always have at the end of school?"

I nodded.

"Well, as you know, the sixth graders put on the play, the fifth graders are in charge of the food, and the fourth graders get to do the decorating. We can transform the lunchroom into anything we want. I'm putting together a committee to decide on a theme and take care of the decorating. I'd like you to be on it."

I beamed. Mrs. Baxter was asking *me*?

"What's the theme?" I asked.

"Anything that you and the committee decide. Feel free to do what you want with it. But find a way to make it special. The choir is going to sing and the band will perform before the play begins. All the teachers and parents will be there."

I remembered the past few end-of-school galas. They're a big deal in our town. Even the mayor comes.

But then I thought about Mom and the service dog and skiing with Becca. And Adam, who always needs my help with math, and the ranch . . . and all the other work. I hesitated. But I just couldn't let Mrs. Baxter down.

"Sure," I said. Where was my "No" when I needed it?

She smiled. "Can you stay after school today and meet with the group? If you start now, you'll have plenty of time to come up with something wonderful."

"Okay. I'll take the late bus home."

She stood up and patted my shoulder. "I knew I could count on you, Nicki."

At lunch, I told Becca about the gala planning group. She looked a little peeved or something, and she pushed her glasses up on the bridge of her nose. "We hardly have any time for skiing or for trips to the mall in Denver as it is."

I said, "I know." Becca and I are also shopping buddies. We work hard at having a unique style, despite being on a budget. Mom, with her artist's eye, is an awesome help to us. I wondered if she'd be able to make trips to the mall anymore.

Becca looked sad about the gala committee. I thought she might have been a little jealous. I said, "I wish Mrs. Baxter had asked you to be on the gala committee, too."

She shrugged and adjusted her ponytail. "It's just more work, which is the last thing I need. You, too."

I slumped in my chair. Becca didn't even know about the service dog yet.

After school, I told Adam to let Mom know that I was taking the late bus home, and then I went back to my classroom. That's when I saw who else was still there. Mrs. Baxter and Heather and Kris, two of the new girls with the big new houses and cell phones and lots of shoes.

I felt like a bowling ball had been dropped on my chest.

They looked at me in the same way I was looking at them. Heather and Kris had come to our school this year and had gained instant popularity. They are always smiling and talking, surrounded by other girls who want to be just like them. Everyone admires them for reasons I can't exactly figure out. When Heather started wearing a cute woolly headband on really cold days, several of the other girls in our class started doing it, too. And two other girls got their hair cut short, like Kris's. Heather and Kris had always ignored me, so why was I here with them? For a minute, I was sort of mad at Mrs. Baxter.

Mrs. Baxter said, "Come around, girls. Time to put your heads together and start planning." She gathered some things from her desk. "I'll leave you now and let you get started on brainstorming. Good luck!" Then she was gone.

I couldn't believe she'd just dump this on us. Me and Heather and Kris? I was going to need more than just good luck.

By the time I had pulled up a desk, Heather and Kris already had their heads together. Neither one of them looked at me.

"I like the idea of a carnival," Kris was saying. She has short, short dark hair and big eyes that make her look as if she had just moved here from another country. Kind of dramatic-looking, like a model.

Heather said, "Yeah, we could blow up balloons

and have popcorn and cotton candy and pictures on the walls of carnival games and rides." Heather has long blonde hair that moves like a silky sheet against her shoulders. She looks as if she had just moved from California. Maybe she had.

"And we could put little carousels around the stage," said Kris. "We could even usher people in wearing clown outfits."

I was wondering how I would get a clown outfit. But it wasn't exactly an original idea anyway, so I said, "I think the gala was done in a carnival theme just a year or two ago, before you got here."

They looked at each other as if they were thinking the same thing. Heather picked up a couple of pencils and started tapping them against the edge of the table. *Rat-a-tat-tat,* over and over.

I'd noticed this habit of hers before, during class. Mrs. Baxter had asked her to stop it a couple of times. But Heather is popular—she seems to get away with anything. Sometimes I wondered what it would be like to do *anything* and have everyone admire you anyway.

They looked at me, finally. Heather's eyes were hard, and she kind of snorted. "Well, it would be *different* if we did it."

I shrugged. "Well, if you're going to use an old

theme, we could get some of the used decorations from the basement. They keep everything down there."

"No way," said Heather and tapped hard. Then she stopped for a moment and moved a sheet of hair back over her shoulder.

Kris shook her head. "Half the fun will be making everything new."

"We could even hire a juggler or a snake charmer or something," Heather added.

"Yeah," said Kris. "That would make it different."

I bit my lip. Where would they find a juggler or a snake charmer? And the school wasn't giving us money to hire performers. I already knew that, because I had been here for so long. We were supposed to do this ourselves, with supplies from the school.

Finally I said something. "Some people are scared of snakes. I don't know if the school would allow it."

Heather squinted at me. "We won't let anyone get *hurt* by the snake. It'd be a tame one."

I shrugged. "Well, I don't know any snake charmers around here, anyway."

They stared at me then.

"What do you have against this idea?" asked Heather. Her eyes were boring into me, and I could feel my face turning red.

"Yeah," said Kris.

It was two against one. Now both sets of eyes were like daggers, and I couldn't escape the smart of them. I hated this feeling.

"Nothing," I finally said in a whisper.

I should've kept my mouth shut. *It's easy*, I told myself. *Just keep your lips closed. With these two, it won't matter what you say, anyway.*

But Heather and Kris started bringing up other ideas—a garden theme, a vacation theme, an animal theme with bugs and butterflies everywhere. Nothing unusual. Nothing different. I knew this was not what Mrs. Baxter was hoping for. But I could already tell that Heather and Kris weren't going to listen to me. Besides, I had zero ideas of my own. This was going to be terrible. *Oh, why did I say "Yes" to this when I should have said "No way!"?*

We finally gave up and left a few minutes later, having accomplished a big nothing.

At home I told Mom about the committee, but she was more worried about the time it would take than about the girls I had to work with. About Heather and Kris, she said, "You never know a person until you spend time with him or her. They might turn out to be really nice after all."

I doubted it. "I wish I had said no. Maybe I should back out."

Mom paused. "But you agreed, right?" She was staring at me. "Now you've made the commitment. How much time is it going to take?"

"I think I'll have to stay late about one day a week, maybe more."

Mom paused and said, "You know the dog is coming, too."

How could I forget?

On Saturday I helped Dad outside early, early in the morning. Most of the work with the pigs is done automatically. Their food and water are supplied by machinery, and even the manure is automatically removed from below the slotted floors of the pens, but we have to supply a good layer of bedding—oat straw—to absorb all the waste. And now it was almost shoat season.

Shoats are young, weaned piglets, which we breed and sell every spring and fall. They have to have vaccinations and health certificates. The piglets are cute, but it's all very complicated and time-consuming.

But after my work was done, I got to go skiing with Becca, and all the stuff that was worrying me fell away like air. Mom and Dad just bought me skis for my tenth birthday, so this spring I have my own skis for the first time and don't have to stop at the rental place.

Becca's mother took off on the black diamond runs, but Becca and I weren't good enough for those yet. We hit the powdery blue runs instead, and as the sun came up, the snow softened so that it was the consistency of sifted flour. Down we went, carving arcs in the snow and flying like there was nothing else in the world.

When we stopped for a break, I said, "Let's try the moguls."

Becca said, "Do you think we're ready?"

"We'll never know unless we try."

When we got to the top of a mogul run, we took off our goggles and looked down. A couple of really great skiers passed us and took off down the bumps, catching big air in between the mounds of snow. They were like birds soaring off the moguls and coming down with a *swoosh-y* crunch on the snow, and then doing it again.

Finally, when the great skiers were gone, Becca and I started down. The moguls sure are bigger when you're in the middle of them! I had to concentrate and really slow down, choosing my course around the bumps that now looked like hills. But I picked my way down and nearly lost it only once, when I started going a little too fast. I accidentally skied up to the top of one massive mogul and then had to ease my way off it. Beyond the moguls, however, it was a deserted blue run all the way down to the day lodge. We didn't stop or fall once from then on, and it was just like flying again, with those narrow wings on my feet.

At the bottom, Becca was grinning, and her eyes were gleaming like shining bowls. I smiled so big, my teeth got dry. I wasn't thinking about Heather and Kris or the service-dog manual I was supposed to read that night when I got home. It was a *perfect* day.

3

The Arrival

Mom woke me up early on Sunday. "I have a gift for you," she said. "It's to help you with the dog."

I was still rubbing my eyes awake. Then, as I stretched out my skiing-sore muscles, it hit me. Right. The dog was coming today. I sat up in bed. Mom was sitting next to me, holding a book in her lap.

"It's a journal," she explained. She ran her hand over its smooth outer cover. "When I first started working with service dogs, my mentor gave me one. In this, you can write down your thoughts and chart the dog's progress. Think of it as a 'dog log.'" She smiled and handed the journal to me. "Did you read the training manuals last night, Nicki?"

I glanced toward my desk. The manuals were stacked there, untouched.

"I was too tired, Mom."

She let out a long breath. "Well, there's plenty of time for that. Today we'll just get to know the dog. While you were on the mountain yesterday, I found out a lot about him." She opened her mouth to say more.

"Not now, please," I pleaded. "I need to wake up."

"He'll be here in an hour."

I wanted to go back to sleep. But I said, "Okay," through a sigh. "Go ahead."

"He's eight months old. The service dog organization found him in a shelter and conducted health and temperament testing. They think he has potential."

Eight months old. I had been hoping for a *real* puppy, a young puppy.

Mom said, "Want to know his name?"

"Sure."

"It's Sprocket."

A little smile rode up my face. "That's a cute name."

Mom patted my knee and smiled, too. I set the journal down on my bedside table and pushed back my covers. Time to get moving, to get ready for Sprocket.

I took a quick shower and then devoured the oatmeal Mom had made. "How are you feeling, Mom?" I couldn't help wondering what it would feel like to have two babies inside of you.

"Very well, thank you. There's nothing like a good night's sleep."

We sat at the table together. As usual, Dad was already outside working, and Adam, the lucky duck, was getting to sleep in.

Before I knew it, a knock sounded on the front door.

When Mom opened the door, I was standing with her. I barely had a chance to glance at the woman who stood on our doorstep, because there was this DOG lunging against his leash, his paws slipping and sliding on the linoleum floor of the entry, and then he was jumping up on Mom's legs. He was MUCH bigger than I had expected. He was brown and black and white with kind of a medium-length coat, not a breed I recognized.

The woman called Sprocket back and reminded him to sit, which he ignored until she finally pushed his rump down. "Sorry," she said. "Sprocket has had an exciting day. And too much time in the car, I'm afraid."

Mom said, "Mrs. Tate, this is my daughter, Nicki." To me she said, "Nicki, this is Mrs. Tate. She's going to be helping us with Sprocket."

I said, "Hi," but I couldn't take my eyes off the DOG. Boy, was I going to need a lot of help. I'd been expecting a *little* puppy until earlier this morning, and Sprocket was a really *big* puppy. He had brown eyes and the cutest puppy face. But he looked kind of scared. His eyes were a little wild. "What kind of dog is he?" I asked.

Mrs. Tate said, "He's a mix. Some people say he looks like a Bernese mountain dog, but we think he's a mix of Australian shepherd, retriever, and maybe some border collie. What's really important is that he's smart. He practically aced all of our intelligence testing."

I was listening, but what really interested me was Sprocket's face. The fur there was soft and white in the middle. He looked so round-nosed and innocent.

"May I pet him?" I asked Mrs. Tate.

She said, "For a bit. But just a little bit."

I crouched down and rubbed the soft fur behind his ears with both hands. I could feel some twitching in the muscles of his neck. But as I rubbed longer, he relaxed and his eyes became softer. I stroked his ears, which were black and silky like velvet. Then, what do you know—he gave me the cutest doggie smile.

When I stood up, all I could say was, "He's bigger than I thought he'd be."

"He's not fully grown yet," said Mrs. Tate. "But almost. He's a teenager dog."

Ugh. A teenager. Becca has a fifteen-year-old sister who is never nice to us. She talks on the phone and tells us to get lost most of the time. But I could see what Mrs. Tate meant. Sprocket looked like a cross between a puppy and an adult dog, and had that long-legged, lean look of a teenager. And despite his jumping up on Mom, I just knew he'd be much nicer than a human teenager.

"Your mother has told me a great deal about you, Nicki," Mrs. Tate said to me. "She tells me that you're a very responsible, compassionate girl. And a natural with animals."

I nodded. *That's me,* I thought. *A very responsible girl with an adorable teenage dog—but a girl who probably should've said NO.*

"Do you think you'll be able to handle some of the training without your mother? I know about the twins." She turned to Mom. "Congratulations, again."

Mom smiled. "Nicki will be able to handle it."

I couldn't take my eyes off Sprocket. He was still sitting but had started pulling and pushing against his leash again, and his tail was going like crazy, making big swipes across the floor.

"I'm available to help, too, Joan," said Mrs. Tate. "Don't hesitate to call. As you know, there are usually some frustrations with each dog. I'll be able to give you advice and come over from time to time."

We all sat down in the living room, Sprocket needing a little help from Mrs. Tate. Then Mrs. Tate started telling me about training service dogs. "Your goal is a well-behaved, responsive young dog ready to begin advanced training. Sprocket should have good manners at home and in public and a good attitude toward carrying out commands."

I felt as if I were in school.

She went on, "The purpose of training with the dog is to learn how to communicate and conduct exercises that can be applied in settings of everyday life. You'll learn how to use motivation and reward with dog treats, and then you'll have to wean the dog off the treats. Finally, you'll teach him social skills."

Mrs. Tate stayed for a cup of coffee with Mom while I followed Sprocket as he sniffed and snooped all over our house. In my room he picked up a dirty sock from the floor and seemed intent on taking it with him, probably to hide and keep as a future chew snack. I know how young dogs are. My aunt and uncle have a dog, and young dogs eat everything. I had to tell him, "Let go," and pull my sock out of his mouth, but not without a little tug-of-war game first.

So much for social skills.

In Mom and Dad's room, he went into their bathroom and started to drink water from the toilet—until I pulled him away. Toilet water was dripping from his mouth. *Yuck.*

But at least I knew he was thirsty, so I went into the kitchen and filled a bowl with water. When I set down the bowl, he was so excited that he stepped on my foot with his big-toed paw.

"Ouch," I said, and then I just stood there and watched while he lapped big droplets of water onto the floor.

Mrs. Tate came in to say good-bye.

"Um, I was wondering," I said. "How did you choose this dog? I mean, he's cute and all, but he seems a little hyper."

"There was and is something special about him. All dogs need training," she said with a smile. "Don't worry. It comes with time and patience. Just get to know him for now, and then tomorrow maybe you can start working on the first command."

I had to look away. I didn't know what the first command was. But give me a break—time and patience? I didn't have enough of either one of those things. Maybe I'd said "Yes" to too many things.

"The first command?" I asked tentatively.

"First you're going to teach him his name. With that, you'll be able to work on attention, response, and basic control with commands. He has the ability to show you all of those things. Just start working on it, using his name constantly," she said.

Mrs. Tate brought in a crate and explained that it was a kind of den for the dog. Sprocket would have to learn to sleep in it at night and take rest periods in it, too. "It helps with housebreaking, and sometimes service dogs' owners have to go out without them. Or they must take them on airplanes or trains, so a dog has to get used to going into his or her crate and staying there for up to six hours."

After Mrs. Tate left, Mom told me, "At first, everything you teach the dog, every command, starts by you saying his name. The first command actually is 'Watch me.' Service dogs have to learn to focus on their owners, over and above all else. Kind of like how kids are supposed to listen to and focus on what their parents say," Mom said with a tired smile. "But you're going to have to read those manuals, Nicki. For now, take off his gentle leader—that's the name of the head collar—and let him rest."

I unclipped the leader, and the noseband and neckband slipped off easily. And that's when I got another good look at Sprocket's face, straight on and close up. He was looking closely at me, too. There was something perky and seriously cute about his face.

His eyes were soft and full of something like—I don't know—SOUL or something, and the hair on his face was fuzzy and soft. And then that round nose, so busy sniffing. I couldn't help it; I liked him right away.

But then, while Mom was busy in her room, Sprocket got all jittery and hyper again, and I didn't know what to do. He was looking at me as if he wanted to tell me something. I tried to play with him. Then I remembered the sock he liked so much, and I thought maybe he needed a chew toy. So I pulled one of my old stuffed teddy bears out of the closet and gave it to him. It didn't help.

"What?" I said.

He just looked up at me, wagged his tail, and let out a little yippy sound.

I threw up my arms in the air. "I don't know what you want!"

A minute later he wet on the kitchen floor. Now I had a pool of dog pee to clean up. While I was mopping, I was mad at *him* and also mad at *myself* for not figuring it out. Of course he needed to go outside. That was what he had been trying to tell me.

When Mom came back, I told her what had happened, and she said, "Oh well."

"Aren't dogs this age supposed to be trained?"

The Arrival

"He's been in a shelter, in a cage. Besides, it sounds like he *was* trying to tell you he needed to go out."

"Oh, yeah, I guess so," I said.

She suggested we take Sprocket outside for toileting and then put him in his crate for a nap. "It's important for a service dog to learn to like his crate, which might be hard for Sprocket since he came from a shelter. So let's work on it, but not force him."

She was right. When we came back inside, Sprocket didn't want to go into his crate.

Mom said, "He needs some toys."

I grabbed the old teddy bear, and this time Sprocket took it in his mouth.

I went back to my room for some other old things of mine, and Mom suggested that I put them inside the crate. Finally Sprocket let me lead him inside, and I closed the door. But after he was in there, he looked out at Mom and me and whined.

Mom said, "We'll have to train him to just relax in there. For now let's just ignore him and let him rest." Mom walked away, but I stayed by the crate for a while. Sprocket whimpered a few more times and then finally lay down with his face on his front paws. When I saw those soulful eyes of his fall to a close and stay closed, I finally left him alone.

As I was looking through the training manuals, Becca called, all excited. "Mom and I are going back to the mountain this afternoon to ski. We can come by and pick you up!"

A burst of something really happy shot through me. "Hold on, I'll ask," I told Becca.

I found Mom in the kitchen doing the breakfast dishes. When I asked her about skiing, she said, "It's your first day with Sprocket. I think you should stick around."

"Mom, please," I said. "It's probably my very last chance to go."

"But you need to get to know Sprocket. We both do. You have school tomorrow, so this will be your only full day with him until next weekend."

"Puh-lease?!"

She hesitated for a second but then said, "I'm sorry, but no, it's against my better judgment."

"Mom."

"I've given you my answer. Sorry."

I just stood there.

"Look," she said. "Adam has math homework again. He's going to need your help." She looked around at the kitchen. "This house needs your help, too. But most of all, there's Sprocket."

The Arrival

I was fuming and trying to figure out a better argument when Dad came in through the back door.

"What's up?" he asked when he saw our faces.

"The dog is here," said Mom, trying to sound perky. "Napping for now."

Dad asked me, "So what do you think?"

"I think I want to go skiing."

He and Mom exchanged a look, *that* look. Then Dad said, "I think that I want to get out of these work clothes." It was Sunday, after all.

I thought about following Dad out of the room and begging him to let me go with Becca, but my parents really hate it when I go from one of them to the other. So I ended up taking the phone back into my room and telling Becca I couldn't go.

I was stuck at home, and all because of a too-playful pup.

While Sprocket rested in his crate, I went back to the service-dog manuals and tried not to panic. In addition to housebreaking him and teaching him his name, we were going to have to work on attention with "Watch me." Then I was going to have to teach a bunch of other commands, one by one. There were "Stand," "Sit," "Stay," "Down," "Wait" (for doorways), and "Here" (to come when called). But that wasn't all. I would have to teach him to ignore objects on the floor and drop items from his mouth. I also had to work on greetings, so that he would sit calmly and politely instead of jumping up on people. I had to get him to learn to go for walks on a loose leash, walking by my side and following my stride. There were so many things to do. I couldn't even read it all; it was too much.

Instead I went back to Sprocket and let him out of his crate. I tried to play with him without letting him get too excited. I scratched him behind his ears and stroked his coat and let him play with an old rubber ball. I always called him by his name, but he didn't always listen to me. When he finally looked at me when I called his name, I told him what a good dog he was and gave him a treat. But the next time I called him, he ignored me.

I wished Mom or Dad would help me, but Dad was on the computer, where he analyzes the cost of doing the business of swine. He factors in the age of the stock, the nutriment content and price of available feeds, and things like that. For the feed he has to vary the formulas based on prices and weight gains and market values. You actually have to be smart to raise pigs, but people who don't know that would never believe it.

Mom was busy, too.

The day passed surprisingly quickly. When I put Sprocket back inside his crate before I went to bed, I sat down on the floor in front of it and stared in. He looked back at me, and I could have sworn I saw sadness in his face. He really did have an expressive face. And I knew just how he felt.

Before I went to sleep, I opened the journal Mom had given me. I wrote:

First day with the dog. He's cute, but this is going to be a lot of work. Why did I say "Yes"? Why do people think I can do this?

Then I thought about the day on the mountain I'd missed. I imagined how much fun Becca had had. How could Mom have refused to let me go? I wrote:

Funny, no one around me has any trouble saying "No."

4

Watch Me

The next day on the bus, Becca was quieter than usual. When I asked, "How was skiing?" she said, "Fine."

When I asked, "How was the snow?" she said, "Spring conditions."

"Really?"

"Good spring conditions," was all she said.

I tried again. "Did you go down the moguls again?"

She shook her head and looked away.

Boy, was she sore that I hadn't gone.

Adam turned around in his seat in front of us. He scratched his head. "I forgot my math homework at home."

"You're kidding," I said. "We worked on that for an hour last night." He turned back, and I saw his shoulders fall.

This day was starting out awful.

As we rode on, I told Becca about Sprocket. I told her that I had to turn an oversized puppy into a dog that would stay calm in all situations, even when distracted. He had to learn to "toilet" on command and not beg for food. He had to remain calm around other animals and when introduced to strangers, and learn to seek direction from me.

Finally she was listening like a friend is supposed to listen, and I could tell she felt sorry for me.

When we got off the bus at school, she turned back to me as we were filing out and said, "I know this dog is a big thing and that you have to help your mom. I just wish you had been there yesterday, that's all."

I had to stay late again to meet with Heather and Kris after school. It was the last thing I wanted to do. I knew the dog was waiting, that Mom would need help with dinner, and that I hadn't even done my morning outside chores yet.

But of course I did it. Heather, Kris, and I stayed in the classroom after everyone left. This time they at least waited until I sat down at the table with them, but within a few minutes they had another idea for a gala theme and didn't ask me a thing.

Heather said, "I like the idea of a garden."

"We could put flowers all over the walls," said

Kris. "And we could use flowerpots and watering cans to decorate the stage."

I remembered that the garden theme had been done before, too, but this time I said *nada*, zip, zero. I was invisible anyway.

Heather said, "We could bring in live flowers in pots—you know, from a nursery."

"And some potted trees," said Kris.

"Fruit trees or flowering trees would be nice," said Heather. She picked up her pencils and started tapping them against the edge of the table again.

"Oh, it could be so pretty!" Kris exclaimed.

Heather stopped tapping for a minute. "Maybe we could even put fake grass on the floor. You know, that Easter grass stuff."

It came out before I realized it. "But people have to walk on the floor."

They looked at me, finally.

I said, "It's just that I don't know if we can put slippery stuff on the floor."

They were still looking at me.

Finally Kris rubbed her forehead under her short sprigs of hair. "She's right about that."

Heather pursed her lips and narrowed her eyes. "So what are *your* ideas . . . ?" I could tell she didn't remember my name.

"Nicki."

"Okay, Nicki, what are your ideas?"

I sat there for a minute. I could've told them about all the other things I had to do right now, and that I hadn't had a moment to think about it. Instead I said, "Well, if you like flowers, what if we made them wildflowers? We could make it more of a mountain meadow than a garden."

Kris looked as if she were thinking about it. But Heather moved her hair back over her shoulder and bristled. "We could never get real wildflowers. Think about it. They're *wild*. As in *wild*flowers?"

Kris looked down, and Heather smiled in a witchy way.

I kept my mouth shut after that.

At home, I plunked my backpack down on the counter and headed for my room, but Mom called from the living room, "Come and see. I've taught Sprocket something."

Sprocket looked up as I went in and then let his tongue hang out. His eyes were like chocolate circles against his black and white face, and I could've sworn they were saying, "Hi!" I had to smile.

Mom stood in front of him and said, "Sprocket, watch me."

At first, he didn't take his eyes away from me, and I thought, *Maybe he likes me. Maybe he missed me while I was at school.*

Mom said it again, more firmly this time. "Sprocket, watch me."

He finally turned to her and focused on her face. Mom reached down and scratched his ears and said, "Good," and gave him a doggie biscuit. Then she said to me, "You try it."

I waited for a second or so and then said, "Sprocket, watch me." He didn't listen at all. It took a long time before he gave me some eye-to-eye contact. But I kept on and on until finally he responded. I sat down on the floor and hugged him and then gave him another doggie snack. *Yum.*

While Mom was making dinner, I continued working with Sprocket on his name and on "Watch me." Even when he didn't look at me the way he was supposed to, he still sniffed around as if he expected a doggie snack anyway.

Mom finally said, "That's enough for one day.

He's doing okay, Nicki, really. Just play with him for a while. Give him some praise and affection."

That was fine by me.

After dinner I helped Mom with the dishes while Dad went back outside to settle the animals for the night. I went out to help him when the dishes were done. Some of the *sows*, the female pigs, were getting ready to *farrow*, which means to give birth, and I had to help Dad get the farrowing house ready. It has to be separate from the other pigs and cleaned with boiling-hot lye solution, followed by a boiling rinse. Then we put down fresh, clean bedding.

He said to me as we worked, "Lots of piglets coming this year." He smiled.

I tried to smile back. "Great."

After we finished with the pigs, I decided to put Sprocket on his gentle leader and take him for a walk. The gentle leader was not always the gentlest thing to get on. I had to get the noseband on first and then the neckband, and then clip it in place, making sure it wasn't too tight. To my surprise, Sprocket just sat there, smiling and letting me do it.

Mom told me to say, "Dress," whenever I did this, and eventually Sprocket would learn to stretch out his neck and point his nose, making it easier for us. She also explained that the gentle leader is sort of like a horse's bridle. It's designed to gently discourage a dog from pulling on a leash with its shoulders and neck, but it doesn't hurt him.

Outside, the stars were glittering chips of light against the black sky. The ranch, the meadows, the pastures, and the huge, huge sky were beautiful on nights like this.

Sprocket, however, wasn't interested in the night sky. He wanted to head for the pigs, but I knew better than to allow that. I led him out toward the pastures instead, but once we got beyond the barn he started speeding up, sniffing the ground like crazy. There are always lots of night creatures in our pastures—field mice, gophers, raccoons, and skunks, to name a few—and Sprocket must have smelled each and every one of them. But he was supposed to be paying attention to *me*.

I tried to control him like I was supposed to. I kept repeating, "Sprocket, watch me," but he wouldn't listen. Oh, what were some of those other commands in the manuals? "Sit" didn't work. My other commands didn't even faze him. He just kept trying to pull, even with the gentle leader. If he could've, he would have dragged me along the ground behind him—and he was much stronger than I expected.

Watch Me

I heard a hawk cry out overhead and then, in addition to pulling and straining, Sprocket started shaking and barking. Boy, his bark was loud!

Woof, woof, woof. Over and over.

I thought I was supposed to say "Quiet," so I tried that, but I couldn't get him to stop.

Woof, woof, woof.

Finally I said, "Shut up!" I couldn't help myself.

Sprocket kept barking and pulling. I kept telling him to hush and be still, but he wouldn't listen to me. I looked back toward the rectangles of yellow light that were the windows of our house.

Oh, please, please! Someone please help me.

It was Dad who came to my rescue. In his typical calm way, he got the dog under control and helped me lead him back inside after Sprocket "toileted" big-time in the flowerbeds where Mom's crocuses were just beginning to come up.

Back inside, I thought the worst was over. But then Sprocket stood at the back window and barked more. I tried to quiet him because Mom was already in bed, but he wouldn't stop. He must have seen or heard or smelled something out there that he wanted. *How do you train that kind of instinct out of a dog?* I wondered.

When he finally stopped barking, I went to

get some juice out of the refrigerator, and Sprocket followed me into the kitchen, as if he was looking for food. Another instinct to train out of him.

We'd been back inside for only a minute, when he "toileted" again, this time on the kitchen floor.

Dad came in, kicked off his boots with a *thunk,* and headed into the kitchen. I opened my mouth to warn him, but not fast enough. His bare feet slipped on the wet floor, and he almost went crashing down. Dad's face turned cherry red as he picked up one wet foot and let it drip. Dad never turns cherry red. He's always Mr. Calm.

"Darn it all," he muttered. I knew he wanted to say more, but I was there.

I said miserably, "He's not even house-trained yet."

Dad managed a tense shrug. "It'll work out. Don't get discouraged, Nick."

But Dad turned red again when he and I had to wait for a long time before Sprocket would go into his crate for the night. I kept giving the command, "Sprocket, kennel . . . kennel," but he wasn't listening.

After Sprocket finally went in there with his toys, Dad wiped his brow with the back of his hand.

"Whew," he said. "Long day."

Wow, was *that* true.

I was tired, but for some reason I sat and watched Sprocket again while he whined in the crate. Something about those eyes kept drawing me in. *You're a silly dog,* I kept saying to him with my eyes. *I don't know if I'm going to be able to do this. I don't know if you're going to be able to do this either.* I felt sorry for us both.

Before I went to bed, I pulled out my journal to write about Sprocket and his progress—or more like his lack of progress. Looking out my window at the black night, I also thought miserably about my school gala group. No progress there, either. Finally I started to write about Sprocket and his crazy barking and about him toileting on the floor. I stopped and looked back at the window, and then I wrote:

No frost on the window. First night without frost. Spring's really here. But with so much going on, I'm not going to be able to do much with Becca when it warms up anyway. It's probably going to be the worst spring ever.

5

Blizzard

I was supposed to do at least three short training sessions with Sprocket each weekend day. We started Friday night. Sprocket was getting better about his name and "Watch me," so I also worked on "Sit." When he wouldn't obey, Mom suggested that I hold a treat over his head.

"He'll naturally follow the treat upward with his eyes and sit."

It worked. Big warm relief spread through me.

On Saturday morning I also had to help Dad with brushing and grooming the horses we stable. I love this job because the horses are such big, beautiful animals. When I finished with the boarders, I turned to my horse, Jackson. Jackson is a gorgeous buckskin, tan and sleek with a dark tail and mane. My favorite thing is to feed him oats out of my hand. I love the feel of his rough tongue on my fingers.

Becca had asked me to go skiing again, saying again that this would probably be the last decent weekend to go, but I'd had to tell her I couldn't go.

"Well," she had said, "I guess I'll ask Emily."

Emily is a friend of ours, but she doesn't go along on our best-friend days. She has her own best friend.

"Emily?"

"Yeah," answered Becca. "She hardly ever gets to go up to the mountain, so she's dying to go."

I couldn't imagine anybody but Becca and me on the mountain together. That was the way it had always been.

"I didn't know Emily could ski," I said softly.

"She's learning, and she wants to get better."

Envy flowed through me, like the flu or something. But *I* couldn't go, so I told myself I should be happy for them.

After working with the horses, I took Sprocket out of his crate, put on his gentle leader, and took him right outside for toileting. He was getting better—no more accidents in the house, at least not for a few days now. After I brought him back inside and fed him, I said, "Watch me."

He did, and when he looked at me, I could have sworn he was trying to tell me something. But what? Or maybe he was just excited about the morning.

I could already tell that he was a morning dog—kind of like a morning person. There was something in those eyes that said, "I like this brand-new day!"

So I worked more on "Watch me," followed by "Sit," until he was starting to sit right away. Mom said he had to learn "Sit" before we could move on to "Down."

He was learning to sit pretty well, but he tended to gulp down his treat, along with all my praise and loving, and then stand right back up to go snooping around the house. I constantly had to go after him. My own legs were starting to ache from getting up and down so often!

When Mom asked me to help with the laundry, Sprocket trotted after me into the utility room, wagging his tail. He stopped and whimpered by the door that led outside, so I stopped what I was doing to take him out for more toileting. But I didn't mind. I was happy that we were communicating so well.

While I was folding towels, he disappeared. I found him in the living room, sniffing around. I called, and he turned around in one fast movement—which was great—but his wagging tail took a swipe across the coffee table—which was not so great. In a split second, his tail knocked everything onto the floor, including

Mom's collection of little painted boxes.

"Sprocket!" I yelped. "You have to be careful with that tail of yours. It's deadly."

Sprocket hung his head, as if he were very embarrassed. I reached out to pet him and reassured him that I knew he hadn't done it on purpose.

I decided that Sprocket needed a walk and some time outside, but I knew that I would have to control him somehow.

I quickly finished with the towels and grabbed Sprocket's leash and my satchel of art supplies. Outside I waved to Dad, who was taking one of the horses for a ride. The horse's coat was shining like brushed suede in the sunshine, and for a moment I wished I could've been riding with Dad instead. I hadn't had any time to ride Jackson since Sprocket's arrival.

It was a perfect mountain spring day. The pastures were clear of snow and starting to show just the tiniest tinges of green. The air was still and cool, but the sun was warm.

Sprocket tried to trot off, but I corrected him in a firm but gentle way, just like I was supposed to do. "No," I told him. "Heel."

Finally he settled down and walked beside me, but he kept stopping to sniff at odors on the ground.

"Sprocket," I told him, "you're supposed to be following along with me. Pay attention to *me*. No! Watch me!"

Instead, he kept doing as he pleased. But I did *not* give up. I kept working on attention and other commands. Finally, I led Sprocket to the one and only hilly spot on our ranch. It's a little collection of hillocks before the foothills really start to rise up behind us, and it's my favorite place to sit and sketch. I got Sprocket to sit down beside me, and I set my sketch pad on my lap. I wanted to come up with something good to paint with watercolors later. But what? This was the same view down the valley I'd always seen. I held the pencil in my hand and stared. It actually felt good to be doing nothing.

Sprocket started breathing hard and looking up at the sky. I followed his gaze.

It was a butterfly, a yellow butterfly. The first one I'd seen this spring. The butterfly was soaring above our heads, and Sprocket was enchanted. His eyes darted every which way to follow the butterfly, and his face opened up into one of those huge grins of his.

I said, "You like that butterfly, Sprocket?" and petted him. I could tell he wanted to go and chase after it, but instead he sat still beside me. Before I knew it, the butterfly came so close, it almost landed on Sprocket's nose. For a second, the butterfly and Sprocket were silhouetted together against the sunlight, nose to nose.

Now I knew exactly what to sketch.

When I was finished, it felt like the best drawing I'd ever done. It was good, Sprocket was good, and I felt warm and happy.

Then, on the way back home, a truck backfired on the nearby road, and Sprocket lost it. He started barking wildly and shaking, and I couldn't get him to stop for a long time. By the time he calmed down and we got home, that warm feeling was gone.

I found Mom stretched out on her bed. I told her, "Sprocket is too much of a puppy."

She said, "In many ways, this training asks a dog *not* to be a dog. You have to train all that impulsiveness out of him. He has to learn how to behave and remain controlled in all sorts of situations."

"He sure doesn't like loud noises," I said.

Mom frowned. "I've noticed that, too." She sighed. "Most dogs have some fear or another. And shelter dogs can be especially unpredictable. You never know what they've been through. But don't worry. We'll work on helping him not be so fearful. For now, let's just work on 'Down.' Then greetings. We can ask your father and Adam to approach Sprocket, and then work with him so that he doesn't get overly excited. No jumping up on people or begging to be petted."

"Why can't he be petted?"

"Well, it's because a service dog has to focus on his owner. He shouldn't get distracted from his work. When you start taking him out in public, people will ask you if they can pet him, and it's up to you to decide. Sometimes you'll say yes, but tell the person that you need to put Sprocket into "Sit" first. Or you might say yes, but tell the person that you might have to ask them to stop if you see Sprocket getting too excited."

"Some people might just come up and hug him. He's kind of cute, you know," I said.

Mom smiled. "You'll have to ask people not to do that, Nicki. It's for the good of the dog. You need to help him succeed, so that he can move on and help someone live a more independent life. Remember, that's the goal here."

I sighed. "Okay."

Later I did ask Adam to approach Sprocket. At first Sprocket tried to lunge at Adam, but I held him back. We did it several times, until Sprocket started obeying me better.

When Dad came in for coffee, I asked him to approach Sprocket.

Sprocket was just as excited as he'd been with Adam. *Oh boy! A new person!* his body seemed to say as I struggled to restrain him. This was going to take a lot of patience!

I reminded Sprocket to sit, and after he was finally listening to me, I gave him a treat and let Dad pet him for a few minutes. At first he behaved calmly, but then he took a big swipe at Dad's hand with his tongue.

I said, "No," and then he did it again. He even tried to chew on Dad's fingers.

Dad was smiling, but I said, "You'll have to stop, Dad. He's not paying attention to me anymore."

At least Dad minded me!

On our second walk of the day, Sprocket did better. I still had to remind him a few times to stop him from sniffing, but I could tell he was learning. I gave him another snack. But instead of taking it gently, as he was supposed to, he just chomped it down.

Please, please, I thought, *let him be a quick learner.*

When we walked past the pig parlor, Sprocket went berserk again. The hogs we sell are kept confined, so Sprocket couldn't see them, but it was probably that odor that set him off. He started barking like crazy and pulling like an ox.

The *boar*, the male hog we keep for breeding, is often outside in his pen. He's a tough fellow, but even he acted alarmed about all the barking. Usually the boar runs back and forth along the fence of his pen, snapping and slobbering, but today he looked freaked. He backed away from the fence, snorting and almost whimpering, as if he was fearful of attack.

I dragged Sprocket inside as fast as I could and decided to put him into his crate for a rest period. I needed a rest, too—or at least a break. Adam was getting ready to go outside to help Dad.

"Want to watch the dog instead, and let me go?" I asked him.

Adam smirked. "No way, José."

That night I got Sprocket settled down on the floor in my room before dinner. I touched the top of his soft head and stroked him for a long time until his eyes blinked shut and stayed that way longer and longer. He seemed to be saying *Thank you*.

I said, "Good dog. Good Sprocket," and left him up there when I went to eat, happy that he was so calm.

At the table, Mom said, "We're making good progress with Sprocket, Nicki, and you've done great work today on your own. I'm so proud of you."

Dad bit into a chicken thigh. "You're doing an important job. I'm proud of you, too, Snicker."

I rolled my eyes. "Snicker" is my dad's pet name for me, but I think I'm getting too old for it. I looked at Adam, who gave me that second-grade smirk of his.

"What's next?" I asked Mom.

She said, "Just keep doing more of the same. But once he learns a command, really learns it, you'll have to stop rewarding him with snacks. After a while you save the snacks for new commands or to reward good behavior in public. But Sprocket needs lots of repetition and encouragement for what he's doing right."

After dinner, warmed by my parents' praise, I walked back to my room, but Sprocket wasn't there. I couldn't hear him anywhere, either.

A really bad feeling came over me. I charged through the house, searching and calling his name. I finally found him in the living room in the middle of what looked like a snowstorm. There were white feathery things everywhere, even drifting in the air.

"What in the world!"

Blizzard

I thought, *What in the world?!*

Then I saw Mom's down vest in shreds on the floor. Sprocket had chewed and wrestled with it, releasing all the teeny tiny fluffy feathery down that had been packed between the layers of the vest. He had found something new to play with—and had created a blizzard in the living room.

Mom came up behind me. I looked helplessly from Mom to Sprocket. Sprocket actually looked pretty pleased with himself, but I'd never seen such a look on Mom's face—it was kind of like the look she gets when Adam or I have disappointed her, only worse.

"Sprocket!" I yelled.

His tail stopped wagging.

"Maybe the stuffed animals weren't such a good idea, Nicki. Now he thinks soft squishy things are for chewing," Mom said finally.

"He's still a puppy, Mom, a big puppy. But . . . how could he do this?!"

I frowned at Sprocket. He looked at me as if he couldn't figure out what he'd done wrong and why I was mad. The look on his face said, *Come play with me—this is fun! And love me; love me, no matter what!* Then he cocked his head to one side as if asking a question.

"He doesn't know any better," Mom said with

resignation. "He just needs a *lot* more training."

We stood in silence then, surrounded by white. Finally Mom shook her head. "Oh, well, now I have an excuse to get a new vest." Then a small smile crossed her face and she said, "Shall we get to work with the snowplow—I mean, the vacuum cleaner?"

On Sunday night, after another long day in which Sprocket made only a little progress, Heather called. She asked in a not-very-friendly tone if I could meet at the public library Monday evening to work on the gala.

I asked, "Why can't we just stay after school?"

"Kris and I are starting a ballet class that meets right after school on Monday, so it has to be later."

"Oh."

"But if you can't make it, that's okay."

I didn't know what to say. Did she even *want* me to make it? Finally I said, "I'll figure out how to make it."

Dad said he could give me a ride back into town. I called Heather back to say that I'd be there for sure.

Maybe this was a good opportunity for me to take Sprocket out for his first public appearance. A library is quiet, which is good. Mom said a better choice might be someone's house, but I hadn't had a chance to go over to Becca's lately. But, we agreed, it was time to start somewhere.

While I was at school on Monday, Mom drove to town and bought some thick, rubbery doggie chew toys. She gave them to me after school, saying that we should teach Sprocket it was okay to chew these things and these things *only*.

Mom also told me that she had visited Mrs. Tate, who had agreed that Sprocket's training was going well enough that he was probably ready for a short public outing. She had also agreed that our town's small public library was probably quieter than many people's homes.

Then, in her serious voice, Mom said, "I went to the doctor today, too." She glanced at me. "It's not a big problem, and I don't want you to worry, but my blood pressure is a little high. Just a little."

"What does that mean?"

She gave me a watery grin. "I guess I'm a little old to be having twins. And the doctor's pretty protective. She wants me to go on bed rest for a while."

"What? You mean you can't get up? Ever?"
I tried to fight against a rising fear in my chest.

"Not exactly. Of course I can get up to go to the bathroom and such. But as for training Sprocket . . ."

"Oh," I said.

Mom sighed and looked down again. "Mrs. Tate said that she can take Sprocket back, if that's what we decide. In fact, she said she would train him herself."

I slumped. I didn't know what to think. I was worried about Mom. Usually when parents tell you not to worry, that's when you worry the most. And then, Sprocket. How could I give him up already?

Mom was studying me. "What would *you* like to do, Nicki?"

I shrugged. "I've been doing a lot of the training anyway. I'll just do it all for a while."

Mom looked away. "Well, it might be a long while. The doctor doesn't know for sure. It all depends on my blood pressure readings."

Just then Sprocket came into my room and put his head in Mom's lap. She started stroking his head. I knew she didn't want to give up on this, and I realized that I didn't either.

I sat up straight. "I can handle it, Mom."

She let out a long breath. "If you change your mind . . . I mean, it's a huge responsibility for a girl your age. You were only supposed to be helping me."

"I can do it."

Dad stuck his head into my doorway. "Here are my two favorite females!" Then he said to Mom, "And what are you doing up?" He gave her a sympathetic smile but tilted his head toward their bedroom.

"Okay, okay, I'm going now!"

"Nicki," Dad said, looking at his old pocket watch as he headed for the kitchen, "let's leave for the library in forty-five minutes. Looks like a storm's coming in fast, but we should be fine. I think it'll blow through just as quickly."

After Mom left, I let Sprocket get up on my bed. I stretched out alongside him and stroked his belly, which he loved.

The wind suddenly picked up, and we heard thundering in the distance. Sprocket's ears perked up like tents. The rainstorm that had been brewing came closer and brought lots of loud rumbles and a few big booms. Before I knew it, Sprocket was shaking and whimpering. I stroked him and talked to him in a low voice and stared into his eyes until his trembling stopped.

I was scared, too. But not of the storm.

Before we left for the library, I pulled out my journal and wrote a quick note about Sprocket:

NICKI

It's like trying to train the little pup out of the big pup. And making him grow up too fast.

Sprocket didn't know how to fit in around our house and ranch and how to cope with the noises of the countryside, just like I didn't know how to fit in with a couple of rich girls who could get away with anything and whose lives were nothing like mine. I thought about the tone of Heather's voice during that phone call yesterday. I could tell that she didn't think much of me, and I didn't know what to do about that. We just didn't click. I wrote:

It was like Heather was forcing herself to call me, because she has to, because of Mrs. Baxter and all. But it felt like a sympathy call.

6

Out in the World

I closed my journal and smiled down at Sprocket at the exact moment that the sun burst through the dark clouds. "You're going out, Sprocket." I reached down and scratched him and rubbed his ears. "The storm has passed and you're going to town." I was happy for him.

Mom got out of bed for a minute, promising that it was okay, and helped me get him ready. "He needs his cape, so that people will know he's in training as a service dog and will allow him inside public buildings," she said. She draped and then clipped the service-dog organization's cape over Sprocket's back. Then we put on the gentle leader. "Be firm with him if you have to. Good luck and have fun!"

She handed me a pack of cleanup supplies to tuck into my bag. "You always have to clean up after the dog, no matter what."

I groaned.

I finished doing as she told me and slung my bag over my shoulder. I felt as if I were carrying a diaper bag. But I led Sprocket out to Dad's pickup truck and helped him jump into the seat, and then we headed to town.

Sprocket was quivering when we pulled up to the library. He was *too* excited; I knew it and had a bad feeling. When I got Sprocket out of the truck, he headed for the grassy area in front of the library, sniffing around, and then, what do you know? He pooped on the library's lawn. I said, "Hurry," the command for toileting, and then, "Good hurry," when he was done.

I looked around. I was thankful that Heather and Kris hadn't arrived yet. The last thing I needed was for them to see me cleaning up dog poop! I quickly pulled out a cleanup bag, scooped up the mess, and disposed of it in the garbage can outside the library.

At the door, I said, "Sprocket, wait," so his paws wouldn't cross the threshold before I had said, "Good."

But inside he wanted to excitedly greet the librarian, Miss Hollister. I was pretty proud of the way I handled him. After only a couple of repeated commands, he was sort of behaving, sitting there panting and smiling, as only dogs can do. But he was shaking a little bit, too, as though he wanted to bolt.

Kris and Heather came in together. Sprocket nudged closer to me.

"What's this?" asked Kris. "Who's this?"

"He's in training to become a service dog. You know, one of those dogs who help people in wheel-chairs and all. His name is Sprocket."

They looked down at Sprocket and smiled, both of them, and started to reach out to pet him.

"Girls, you need to ask his trainer if you can pet him," said Miss Hollister gently. Our librarian knows everything.

Kris said, "May I?"

"Sure," I answered.

She and Heather, who hadn't bothered to ask, crouched down on the floor and gave Sprocket a nice little love session, with lots of pats on the head and scratches behind the ears. He was doing okay—he tried to lick Kris's hand once, but when I said, "No," he listened and obeyed, for a change.

"Wow," said Kris. "This is way cool. You know how to train service dogs?"

"Well, actually I'm just learning. My mother used to do it."

Even Heather was nice. "He's adorable."

But then she set her backpack down on the floor, and Sprocket grabbed it with his teeth. Before I knew it, Heather was pulling back on the backpack, and a game of tug-of-war had begun. I knew from reading the training manuals that tug-of-war is not a good game for a service dog in training. It can encourage aggressive behavior. And I could see it happening already. Sprocket was getting agitated, squirming and digging in his heels as he pulled. He was even starting to growl. He thought this was a fine game!

Heather and Kris did, too. They laughed as Heather tugged back.

I opened my mouth to say something, but nothing came out. The words just vanished from my tongue.

Okay, so what was I supposed to do? For once, Heather and Kris thought something I was doing was interesting. I guessed that they liked the dog more than they liked me, but I needed to make Heather stop.

Miss Hollister saved me again. "Heather, that's not a good idea. This is a dog training to become a work dog. My neighbor has a seeing-eye dog, so I know something about this. Better stop. Okay?"

"It won't hurt anything. Can't I just play with him a little more?"

Miss Hollister said, with firmness, "Better not."

Heather looked peeved, but she did as Miss Hollister asked.

I felt embarrassed that I hadn't said anything to stop her, that I'd just let the librarian handle it.

We found a table, and I got Sprocket to go down under it next to my feet. He put his head across his front paws and just chilled for a while. I was proud of him for that.

Kris said, "I'm beginning to like your idea about the mountain meadow, Nicki."

I couldn't believe it. She remembered my name. And she liked my idea.

But Heather piped in, "I don't think there's enough there. I mean, what's in a mountain meadow except for grass and wildflowers?"

Kris looked my way. I shifted uncomfortably in my chair. "Well, there are all kinds of wild animals, and birds in the sky," I said. "There's usually a stream running through a meadow."

Heather said with a smirk, "How could we make a stream?"

I just sat there. I had no idea.

"Forget the stream," said Kris. "We could cover the ceiling with blue paper and hang a big sun from it. And then we could put paper grass on the walls with wildflower cutouts sticking up out of the grass."

"And we could throw in a few animals peeking out, too," I said.

Kris smiled. At least the two of us were on the

same page—finally!

Heather gave a little snort. "There isn't much to it," she said. "I think it's kind of plain."

I sat and thought about past gala themes. All of them had been bright and sunny in one way or another. I hated to say it, but Heather was right about our idea being sort of ordinary.

For the rest of our meeting time, we made no more progress. We just sat and looked at each other, and for a moment I thought I was going to fall asleep. Then Heather picked up some pencils, which she always seemed to have with her, and started that pesky tapping against the edge of the table. *Rat-a-tat-tat.*

All of a sudden Sprocket was on his feet. His eyes looked a little wild. Wow, he didn't like *that* noise, either.

I said, "Sprocket, watch me." He looked, and I stroked him for a moment, long and slow, until I could see the anxiety leave his eyes. Then I told him to sit and finally to go down again. I gave him a doggie biscuit, and I felt pretty good about the way I'd handled him. Luckily, Heather had stopped the drumming.

But he had listened! He was learning to listen to me, and I was learning how to calm him down, even when he got nervous.

As for Heather, Kris, and me, we tried to come up with new and different ideas for the gala theme. But if one of us liked an idea, the other two didn't. It was beginning to feel hopeless.

Finally, we gave up for the night and packed up our papers, no further ahead than when we'd started.

As we were leaving, Sprocket nearly charged a couple of little kids who were on their way in. I had to pull him back, but I was so surprised that it took me a second or so to react. Just when I thought he was making such great progress, he fooled me again. And just when I thought *I* was making progress in my training, I fooled myself, too. It wasn't so easy for either of us.

At home, Mom was in bed, as she was supposed to be, even though it was only 8:00. When I went in to see her, she showed me her ankles, which were all puffy.

"What happened?" I asked her. Not something else!

"It's nothing serious. Just something that happens from time to time when a woman is pregnant. It's a little swelling, that's all."

I just stared at those thick ankles.

"I'm sorry, Nicki, but I have to ask you to do the dinner dishes. And Adam needs help with his math."

I wanted to scream with frustration—and worry.

The smell of something like chili wafted through the house. "Did you get up and cook?"

"Relax," she said. "Your dad made chili while you were at your meeting. You know, dads can do that sometimes."

"Can't they clean up, too?"

Mom smiled. "Nicki, please. He's had a long day."

Now I was losing it. "Well, so have I." But I was embarrassed that I was acting so bratty.

"What happened?"

I sighed. Then I ended up telling her about the gala planning that wasn't going anywhere and about how Sprocket had charged toward a couple of kids at the library right after I'd thought he was doing so well.

"But he otherwise behaved well in the library?" she asked. "He followed your commands?"

I nodded.

"Nicki, you don't know what a giant step you've taken with him. That's great!" She patted my knee and said, "One little slip-up doesn't ruin an entire outing."

"I guess not," I said. And I started to feel a little better.

After I did the dishes, helped Adam, and was finally starting my own homework, Becca called. She wanted to talk about Emily.

"She's getting better at skiing," said Becca. "And next year she's going to get her own skis for Christmas. She practically begged her parents."

"That's cool," I said quietly. Emily is nice and all, but she's never been one of our closest friends. Now all I was hearing out of my very best friend was "Emily this" and "Emily that."

I said, "I ought to go to bed now. Sprocket and I have had a big day."

"What did you do?"

"I met with my gala group at the library and took Sprocket along."

Silence. I thought that Becca and I had gotten disconnected for a minute. She finally said, almost in a whisper, "I haven't even met Sprocket yet."

Oops.

"You spend all your time with Heather and Kris now," said Becca.

"Not really. It's just that I have to work with them on this project."

"Or with the dog."

"Well, that's true. But I have to do that, too."

Finally we ran out of things to argue about. So I suggested, "Come over tomorrow after school. You can meet Sprocket. You'll like him. And you can help us practice greetings and getting to know new people."

Becca waited for a long minute. "Okay," she finally said. "I'll think about it. 'Bye."

I didn't have time to worry about this anymore. Instead, I did my own math assignment and then started on a report that was due in two days. I worked until my eyelids were like lead weights.

The last thing I did was write in my journal:

Sprocket has so much to learn yet. He's responding well to most of the commands I've taught him. He even goes into his crate at night without hesitating now. I see progress, but it's slow.

And then for me:

Sometimes you have so much to do that you end up not doing a good job at any of it.

7

Old Friend, New Friend

Becca did come over after school the next day, and Sprocket behaved well when he met her. No more overexcited greetings! I gave him a special doggie snack, one that looks sort of like a pig wrapped in a blanket, which he gulped down.

I said, "Good dog."

Becca smiled down at him, and I could tell she liked him. I mean, with that face, how could anyone *not* like him, even though he could be such a brat?

Becca and I took him for a walk on the road, and he tried to pull only once.

Mom had told me that I could let Sprocket play once in a while, as long as I supervised him, so I said, "Release," and gave him a little more room to explore on the leash.

But I kept hold while Sprocket sniffed up and down the road. There was barbed-wire fencing along the way, so I kept him away from that. He kind of moseyed, checking things out, but he didn't bark. When he turned around to look at me, he was all tongue and tail. I couldn't help grinning at him.

Looming over us, the mountains were beginning to lose their snow. I stopped to give Sprocket another snack as a reward for his good behavior. This time when I crouched down, he took the snack gently, and then he looked at me and didn't move. Finally he gave me the lightest little lick with his tongue.

It was a kiss, no doubt about it. All of a sudden something began to sting my eyes.

"This is a pretty awesome thing to do," Becca said. "I have to admit it. And he really *is* a cute dog." She gestured toward Sprocket. "But when will it be over?"

Over? I stood up and had a hard time focusing for a minute. Of course someday it would be over. I gulped hard. I knew Sprocket liked me. He trusted me. And now I liked him, too, I mean *really* liked him. So, why *was* I doing this—all for him to end up with someone else?

I finally answered, "We'll have him for about six or seven more months. Then in the fall, if he's done well enough, he'll be sent for advanced training with the service-dog organization."

"And that's it? Good-bye?"

"Unless he doesn't pass the advanced training, it's good-bye. But if he doesn't pass, and that's up to the experts at the organization, we get first choice on adopting him as a pet."

Sprocket glanced back at us, panting and smiling. I noticed that he had grown a little bigger. His paws were even thicker, if that was possible, like tubby paperweights. And his face looked more adorable than ever as he got older.

Walking on, Becca and I talked about school and skiing—not a word about Heather and Kris, or Emily. Then she said, "You know this weekend is absolutely, positively the last time we could go up to the mountain. The ski area is closing after Sunday."

I looked away.

She said, "I know you probably can't go. I just thought I'd mention it anyway."

I didn't want to make any more promises that I couldn't keep, so I didn't say anything.

Later that week, my parents must have been feeling sorry for me. Dad helped with Sprocket's loose-leash training outside. We worked on U-turns and the "Here" command. Mom's blood pressure was better, according to the doctor, but her ankles swelled every night now, and she still had to get lots of rest. So she helped with Sprocket's commands from her perch in bed or from the couch.

In return, I fed the horses at night for Dad, and on Thursday I helped him with one of the boarded horses that had gotten a huge thorn stuck deep in the skin near the bottom of her leg. The mare was kind of fighting us, because she was in pain. Dad told me to be careful and to stand back, just to hand him his tools. But the mare started whinnying and stomping, and it took us a long time to calm her down and get the job done. By that time, I had horse dung on the bottom of my boots and straw sticking to my jeans.

Afterward I took a long hot shower to make sure I got rid of the smell of pig *and* horse. When I finished, I groomed Sprocket's coat and brushed his teeth. I was beginning to like these kinds of things, and I sensed that Sprocket liked to look his best. Now when I groomed him, he sat very still. I teased him in a soft voice. "You know you're handsome, don't you, Sprocket?" I said, and then "You're a big rock-star dog, aren't you?"

Mom called me into her room after I took Sprocket out for his final toileting of the night.

"I think you deserve a day off, Nicki. Why don't

you go ahead and go skiing with Becca this weekend? I know you want to go."

"Really?" I said, beaming.

"Sprocket can take a day off, too. He's doing so well now, Nicki, and it's all because of you."

"Thanks, Mom."

"Thank *you*, sweetheart. Now," she said, patting my knee, "give me a hug and then off to bed with you."

Saturday morning, Becca and I were on the mountain again, just as before. The wind was cool in our faces, but the sun was warm, and we even had to take off our jackets as the day went on. We saw some-one skiing in only a pair of shorts and a light wind-breaker. Spring had come and started to pounce on us.

"How about the moguls?" I suggested.

"Okay," Becca answered. "Emily and I did them that day you couldn't go." Then she looked sorry she had said it. "It was fun all right, but you should have been there, too."

We rode over to the mogul run and watched as some of the great skiers ran it first. It was fun to watch, but it seemed as though they were never going to leave.

"Let's do it anyway," said Becca.

"I'm in," I said, adjusting my goggles.

We waited at the top of the hill for a break in the action. Then we carved and bumped down the course, faster than before. I thought the experts would be looking at us, scrutinizing us, or even laughing at us, because we weren't very fast or skilled yet, but no one acted weird at all. It was as though we fit in, like maybe we belonged there.

When we finished the mogul run, the air tasted like freedom or something. We skied down to the day lodge for lunch.

"Last day," Becca said, but she didn't look sad anymore. "*Really* the last day."

"Yeah," I said. "But think about how much better we skied this year."

She said in between bites, "I bet Heather and Kris don't know how to ski."

"Not yet," I said.

"Yeah, but by next year, they'll probably be taking private lessons."

"We'll still be one step ahead."

"I know," said Becca, smiling. "Before they get to be any good, we should take them on the moguls."

I had to smile.

Old Friend, New Friend

"Only kidding," said Becca.

"Actually, Kris is turning out to be kind of okay, believe it or not."

Becca said, "That's good." But I didn't know if she meant it.

After lunch we skied the mountain like there was no tomorrow. And there really *was* no tomorrow this time. Last day of the season. My skis would have to go into the barn and collect dust for seven months. No more challenging the moguls and hanging out, if not *with* the great skiers, at least close to them.

The day got better and better. Blue sky overhead, white powder on the slopes, green trees all around, warm sun on my face, and fresh mountain air that flowed into me, sweet on my tongue.

And no one to get in the way of Becca and me.

But as we were making our last runs, the weirdest thing began to happen. I couldn't stop thinking about Sprocket. I missed him. It was almost the way I'd felt when Becca went on a long vacation last summer.

After Becca's mom dropped me off, I let Sprocket out of his crate and let him give me a few wet dog kisses on my face. He squirmed a little because he was so excited to see me, but he calmed right down when I told him to sit.

I gave him a bowl of food and restrained him for a moment so that he would know to wait for permission. He obeyed, and then I said, "Okay." While he was wolfing down the food, I could see that his eyes were saying, *Thank you.*

"No more socks or vests," I told him.

He stopped eating for a minute and looked up at me with those soulful brown eyes of his. He cocked his head to one side, something that was beginning to make my chest ache whenever he did it. I lingered with him for a long time, just talking and stroking his head. When he finished eating, he looked up at me with one of those big doggie grins—and then he burped!

That night I wrote in my journal about skiing and about how everything seemed okay with Becca again. Then I wrote about Sprocket. As I was writing about how well he was doing, I had to stop. The page got all blurry, and something was stinging my eyes. I remembered talking to Becca earlier in the week about how someday he was going to leave. I wrote:

He's like a new best friend to me. How will I ever give him up?

8

Gaining Ground

Two weeks later I couldn't believe how much progress Sprocket had made. But then again, I *could* believe it. He was the smartest, sweetest dog in the world. Mrs. Tate had come over to check on him, and afterward, even *she* had said she was pleased.

Now whenever I took him outside, he paused and waited at the door until I told him, "Okay." Even on his long leash he didn't pull anymore, except on the rare occasions when something just demanded his attention, such as when he sniffed out a field mouse in the barn or when he first saw our cattle grazing near the house.

But now he could "Sit," "Stay," and go "Down" on command, and he went into his crate willingly at night and for rest times. He didn't even chomp down his treats—his favorites still the pigs-in-a-blanket—until I told him it was time.

"He's probably going to make a good service dog," Mom told me that Sunday night at dinner. "And you deserve the credit for that."

Dad said, "You've done a *really* great job, Snicker."

"Probably?" I said to Mom.

"Well, there's still more work to be done. We have to work with longer leashes and more advanced commands and discipline."

"I have a question," I said.

"Shoot," replied Mom.

"Do dogs like Sprocket sometimes kind of reach their top form? I mean, kind of stop getting any better?" Under the table I was picking at my fingernails. I didn't know what I wanted Mom's answer to be.

"Sometimes," Mom said reassuringly. "But Sprocket shows no signs of plateau-ing."

"Plateau-ing?" said Adam with a frown. "What does that mean?"

Mom answered, "Reaching a certain level and then not going any further."

"What would happen then?" asked Adam. I was glad he was doing the asking. I could tell that he was getting attached to Sprocket, too.

"All dogs like Sprocket, unless they have major health or behavior problems, go to advanced training with the service-dog organization. In this area, Mrs. Tate does most of the advanced training. Then she'll make the final decision."

"What final decision?" asked Adam.

Mom answered, "About whether or not he can actually work as a service dog."

"And go away?" Adam scooped up some more macaroni and cheese and then just stared at Mom.

She finally answered. "Yes, but go away to help someone who needs him—more than we do."

Silence. Even Adam wasn't moving.

"What does he have to learn to pass advanced training?" I finally asked.

"Things like how to pick up items off the floor, hand money to a cashier, fetch a soda from the refrigerator, turn the lights on and off. Some dogs that show sensitivity to sound learn to act as "ears" for someone who can't hear. They learn how to respond to doorbells, oven timers, alarm clocks, and phones—things like that."

I had no idea if Sprocket could learn that stuff. But he *was* smart; we all knew that now. Maybe he *could* learn anything.

When I took my next bite of macaroni and cheese, the food almost got stuck in my throat, and I had a hard time swallowing it down.

On Tuesday I met with Heather and Kris after school. We were talking about the meadow theme again when I realized something. Heather had complained that it was sort of plain, which was true.

I sat up straight and said, "What if we did this as a summer meadow *night* theme? Instead of blue sky, we could make it dark and put some of those glow-in-the-dark stars on the ceiling. We could hang a moon instead of a sun. And we could make night animals peeking out from the grass. No one has ever done a night theme. No one has ever used night creatures."

Kris was thinking hard, and then she smiled. "I like it. The lights will go down during the play anyway, and it'll feel like a real summer night."

Heather was silent for a minute, but then she said, "It's okay."

"Really?" I said.

She shrugged and moved her hair over her shoulder. "Like I said, it's okay. And we have to start on something. Mrs. Baxter was asking me today what we had come up with, and I had nothing to tell her. At least we have something now."

Mrs. Baxter had asked me about what we had, too, and I hated to see the disappointment in her eyes when I said, "We have no ideas yet."

"Not even a general one, not a theme?" she'd asked.

Heather was still complaining. She said, "We still have no ideas for the area in front of the stage." She sighed. "I mean, what could go across the mountain meadow at night?"

Kris scratched her short hair and sat up straight all of a sudden. She looked at me. "Do you remember how once you mentioned a stream?"

I nodded. "There's usually a stream running through a meadow."

"Well, what if we made a stream out of aluminum foil that ran across that empty area in front of the stage? It would be all silvery, like it was lit up by the moon at night."

I thought about it. "That's a great idea."

"We could even decorate the stream with some pretty rocks and peak up some little waves out of the foil," said Kris enthusiastically.

I said, "I like it. I like it a lot."

Again Heather shrugged. "It's okay . . ." and then, "Fine by me. We have to do *something*."

But Kris and I couldn't stop smiling.

We pounded out some more details on the idea of the night meadow, and then I had to leave to catch the late bus. Kris suggested that we talk on the phone later that night to come up with more ideas.

Heather said to Kris, "I'll call you," and she ignored me. I had already sensed that the two of them had held some private conversations about the gala without me.

Kris said, "Let's do a conference call, with all three of us on the phone at once."

Well, at least I was being included, but I wasn't sure how to do a conference call. I remembered hearing Dad do it with his suppliers, so I knew I could ask him. But still I hesitated. I had so much to do that night.

"What?" asked Heather.

"Oh, nothing. It's just going to take me longer to get home than it will take you guys."

"Okay, so you call me," said Kris. "Then I'll dial in Heather."

So it was set. I couldn't believe that Kris really liked my idea and that Heather, who wasn't exactly thrilled, was at least going along with it.

That night Mom told me that her blood pressure was normal again and she was feeling well enough to drive me to the mall in Denver on Saturday so that we could get some baby stuff and find some summer things for me. Mom said that Becca could go with us, so I flopped down on my bed and called her.

She said, "No, I can't. Too much to do."

Something was wrong. I hadn't done anything with Becca in a long time, and I could sure tell. I said, "Come on, really?"

"Of course, really."

"What's going on?" I asked.

"The usual chores."

"But you've always been able to get out of some chores. Can't you try?"

She made a grunting sound. "You should talk. You spend all of your time with Heather and Kris on the gala project, or else you're training Sprocket. Or doing your chores."

"But I'm going to the mall on Saturday, and I'm asking you to go with me."

"No thanks," she said in a tone of voice that was almost snooty. I'd never heard that tone from Becca before.

"Thanks a lot, Becca."

"Well, you've been telling me 'no' for the past month now."

"But I *went* skiing. And the rest of the time I *had* to say no. My parents made me."

Becca sighed. "I really have too much to do."

I didn't believe her. This felt like payback. "Well, thanks, again," I said.

She said, "You're welcome."

"You're welcome, too."

"You're welcome, three."

Oh boy. I almost hung up on her, but it *was* true that I'd had little time for her. Becca was peeved at me, and that was the last thing I needed.

After I washed the dinner dishes, worked with Sprocket, folded laundry, and then helped Adam with his math homework, it was 9:30, a half hour past my bedtime on school nights. I was looking for my journal when I remembered that I had never called Kris and Heather as I was supposed to. I really didn't need them mad at me, too.

I flopped down on my back in bed and stared at the bleak beige ceiling above me. Then, after a few minutes of feeling sorry for myself, I pulled out my journal and started writing.

How could I have forgotten to call? Heather and Kris are finally getting interested in me, and then I go and blow it by not doing what I had promised to do. Great.

9

Jackson

The next day at school, I decided that as soon as I saw Kris and Heather, I would apologize for not calling them. They were standing outside the door, talking to each other, and I just strode right up.

When I explained that I had forgotten to call, Kris smiled and said, "That's okay. We talked for only a minute."

But Heather threw back her hair and said, "We couldn't get much done without our third member, you know. We're supposed to be doing this together, I mean, like a team?"

Something nearly exploded inside my chest. How unfair was that comment! What did she know about teamwork? She was the one who was always disagreeing with everything.

I put my hand on one hip. "I have no problem working as a team. I just forgot, that's all."

Heather snorted. "Fine."

And I said, "Fine," back. I was tired of Heather pushing me around.

The rest of the day stunk.

But on Saturday, Mom and I went to the mall in Denver. Dad and Adam watched Sprocket while we were gone, so it was just the two of us. We even ate lunch out, in the mall's food court. It was rainy outside and felt almost as cold as winter again, but we bundled up for the drive, talking and listening to the radio the whole way. At the stores, we found a couple of cute new things for me, and they were even on sale! It was so nice to have Mom's energy back—I realized how much I'd missed her regular self.

On Sunday, after working with Sprocket for a while, I rode with Dad to help him check the cattle. He'd been driving hay out to them in the truck until recently, but now that the pastures were greening up, he'd let them go a few days without anything to supplement the grass. He had to make sure they were eating enough to keep their bulk up. It was also a good way to exercise the horses.

I saddled Jackson, and Dad rode his favorite mare, a horse that was as bright as copper and as lively as the fall winds in the pastures.

Fall? What am I doing? I thought. *Fall's when Sprocket will leave. Don't even think about fall!*

It was a super-beautiful, mid-May day. A brief rainstorm had blown through, replaced by sunshine.

Jackson

We could wear short sleeves. I wore my favorite straw hat to shield my face from the sun. It was clear and warm, and even with my hat, I had to squint against the light.

We headed over the pastures that were a little mushy with spring runoff and the recent rain. At the edge of a great open meadow dotted with early yellow wildflowers, Dad and I reined in.

He turned to me. "Want to run them?" I'd been riding horses since I was little, and Dad knew that Jackson was safe and gentle.

I wasn't afraid. "Sure," I said with a grin.

I tapped my heels into Jackson's sides, and he took off. Then Dad and I were flying side by side across the meadow, and my heart was thumping at the same pace that the horses' hooves were pounding the ground. I stood tall in the stirrups and let the warm air flow over me like moving sunlight.

It was almost as good as skiing. Almost.

On the other side of the meadow, we reined the horses to a halt. I was laughing and didn't even know it.

Dad was smiling. "It's good to see you laugh, Snicker," he said, looking over at me.

I grinned bigger.

"You haven't been doing much laughing lately."

"Sprocket makes me laugh."

"What about Becca?"

I squinted against the glare of sunlight. "She's mad at me right now."

Dad waited for a minute, still checking me out. "I'm sorry to hear that, but I'm sure the two of you will work it out."

I said nothing.

"Won't you?" he asked.

I nodded, because I hoped so.

That night Kris called me. Naturally I thought it had something to do with the gala planning, but instead she asked me to come over for Sunday dinner with her family.

For a minute I was speechless. This girl, this girl who had no idea about my life, and who had not been very welcoming to me in the beginning, was turning out to be kind of decent, maybe even nice. And now she wanted me to come over? Like a friend? I didn't know what to say. It was hard to trust someone who had once been kind of mean to me.

She went on, "My father is marinating his famous steaks, and my mother will be making salad and her great twice-baked potatoes."

I wanted to go. Kind of. Maybe I wanted to see what her life was all about. What would it be like inside those tall log-and-glass houses that hugged the hillsides? But I knew it was impossible.

"I'd really like to," I said. "But I can't."

She said, "Why not?"

I hesitated. Even though I wanted to like her a little bit now, I still didn't know if I trusted her. I couldn't tell her that I was the one making dinner at my house that night. Mom had been doing better for a while, but today the swelling had returned. And Dad couldn't do it. Earlier, after we had found the cattle, he'd decided that they needed more sustenance, and so he had headed back out in the pickup to deliver hay. Adam was writing his first paragraphs for school, and I had homework to do, too. And I hadn't done enough in the way of training Sprocket today.

Kris finally said, "That's okay. We'll do it another time." She sounded as if she meant it. So, maybe she did.

I said, "Thanks for asking. I really would like to come sometime."

"I'll keep asking until you say 'okay.' Okay?"

"Sure. See you tomorrow."

As soon as I hung up, another weird thing happened. The phone rang again, and this time it was Heather calling me. She said, "I'm calling to remind you that we're meeting at *my* house tomorrow night."

I knew this already. We were planning to meet after her and Kris's ballet lessons. "I remember. I'll be there. Thanks for calling, though."

"Bring Sprocket," she said, almost as if she were issuing an order.

I stopped for a second. Why did she want me to bring Sprocket? Oh yeah, she liked him better than she liked me. "Okay," I said. "Sure."

"See you then."

After we hung up, I put the phone down slowly.

Jackson

It was odd. I had been thinking of bringing Sprocket anyway.

That night in my journal I wrote:

Becca is mad at me. But Kris likes me now—or maybe she does. And Heather likes my dog. I don't know if I like any of this.

10

A Big Word

Heather and Kris and I were supposed to meet at Heather's at 6:00, and I was dreading it. I wouldn't have minded going over to Kris's, but Heather's?

Anyway, I went, because that was what I was supposed to do, even though we had completed most of the planning for the gala. But it was only a couple of weeks away, and there was still work to do. So I told Sprocket that we were going on a special visit. It would be his first time in another home.

I remembered what he had done to Mom's wooden box collection and hoped his tail wouldn't clear off Heather's coffee table, too. But he was listening to me so much better lately that I was only a little bit nervous for him. I was almost more nervous for *me*.

Dad drove us to Heather's house in the pickup truck. It was a great May evening; spring had fully bloomed. Everywhere the trees had leafed out, and people's flower gardens held bright smears of color.

We had no problem finding Heather's place. The house was outside of town and so big that it stuck out from the mountainside like a shining jewel. Dad gave me a funny look as Sprocket and I got out. "Wow," he said. "I haven't seen one of these so close up before."

I just nodded.

Heather greeted me at the door. She was smiling, I mean really smiling, both at Sprocket and at me.

I told Sprocket to wait before crossing the threshold, and he minded me like magic. Inside, I couldn't believe the house. It had polished wood floors that looked as though they'd never been walked on, and everything was pale blue and beige. It looked like one of the model homes that Mom had decorated in a new Denver subdivision that stretched our way.

I led Sprocket gently over that floor. I didn't want his claws, which I kept trimmed, to scratch that flawless wood.

Heather led the way. We sat down at a table in her family's breakfast nook. I could see into the kitchen, which had an island big enough for a restaurant in the middle. On the wall was what Heather said was a pizza oven, and it was puffing out some great scents. I'd never seen a pizza oven in someone's house before.

Sprocket settled down nicely at my feet under the breakfast table, and then, after Kris arrived, we started working on the lists of supplies we needed to make all the decorations for the gala. We finalized the lists of teams and decided to pass them out at school the next day. One team would work on the ceiling and another team would work on the walls and another team would make the stream in front of the stage.

"What if some kids don't like the team they're on?" asked Kris.

I said, "We could let them switch."

Even Heather agreed. "Yeah, let's be democratic."

Wow.

"Do we need to set deadlines for the work to be finished?" asked Kris.

"We'd better," I said. "Just to make sure it all gets done in time."

Heather nodded. "The gala is on a Saturday night, so maybe we should say that all the decorations need to be up by Friday afternoon."

"Yeah," said Kris, "that way, if something isn't right, we'll have a day to fix it."

I smiled. I couldn't have agreed more. This was turning out okay after all.

We made supply lists for each team and did assignments. Then Heather got up and came back from the kitchen with sodas. "My mother is making a pizza to celebrate. It'll be done in a minute."

I was surprised that she wanted me to stay and

not just Kris. While we ate the really awesome pizza, Sprocket rested under the table. But he lifted his head when Heather brought more to the table. I told him to stay and gave him a doggie treat out of my bag, and he settled down again. He was acting close to perfect, even in this fancy house with all the great-smelling food. I was so proud of him.

Heather's cell phone rang. I let Kris pet Sprocket while Heather talked. I heard her say, "Yeah. Now." When she hung up, she said, "Marcy and Amanda are coming over."

Two other rich and popular girls. I looked at her, puzzled. "What for?"

"We need to celebrate, I mean really celebrate. We'll have a party in the basement. Come and see."

We followed her into the basement, Sprocket at my side.

Heather had an enormous basement done just for her. I guess she really liked music, because the whole thing was done with a music theme. Maybe that was why she was always tapping those pencils like drumsticks. There were pop-group posters on the walls, lamps that looked like guitars, and beanbag chairs covered in fabric that looked like music sheets.

Heather said, "Do you want to hear my stereo?"

Well, I wouldn't have minded hearing it, but I didn't know if Sprocket would like it. He was better about noises lately, but I wasn't sure how he would react. I almost said, "No," but then Heather touched a few buttons, and we were blasted by loud music.

Sprocket cowered. I crouched down to calm him. He settled down a bit, but not enough. I asked Heather to turn down the volume, and she sighed heavily.

Then Amanda and Marcy arrived. Marcy ran up to Sprocket, and just as I opened my mouth to say something about waiting, Sprocket jumped up on her legs.

She was wearing jeans, so it didn't hurt her, but I couldn't get Sprocket back under my control. He was shaking all over.

While I tried to calm him, Heather told Marcy and Amanda that Sprocket was in training, and that was why he was wearing the cape. She talked about him as if she were the expert. They seemed impressed, but I couldn't enjoy their interest, because Sprocket was starting to yip and paw the carpet. I knew that I should get him out of there, but I sort of wanted to stay, too.

I crouched back down to calm Sprocket. But then Heather turned the volume back up, and the others talked and danced. When Heather's mother came down with another just-baked pizza, Amanda grabbed a piece of pizza and headed our way. "Sprocket," she said. "That's the cutest dog's name I've ever heard."

I couldn't take credit for that. "Well, I didn't name him. The service-dog organization did that."

Then Amanda leaned down and gave Sprocket a piece of pizza. Oh no! I tried to stop him from taking it, but it was too late. It was gone in one big gulp.

Okay, so that wasn't good, but Sprocket calmed down a bit. For a few minutes, I felt comfortable, almost relaxed. Maybe this could work. And maybe I was making four new friends, too.

Then Sprocket broke away from me and went for another slice of pizza that Heather had left on a plate on the floor. I went after Sprocket, but once again I was too late. I tried to explain that Sprocket wasn't allowed to eat "people food," but the girls thought it was hilarious. The only one who seemed to understand what was happening was Kris. But she didn't say anything to help me out.

All my good feelings went away. I said to Heather, "I need to call my dad to come and pick us up."

"Oh, come on, Nicki. This is a celebration. We want you to stay, both of you."

"I'm not supposed to let him get this excited. He's doing things he's not supposed to do," I said.

Heather's face changed.

I explained, "All this noise and running around, eating people's food . . . it hurts him with his training. It could hurt his chances of becoming a service dog."

Heather slumped down in a beanbag chair, and she looked as if she didn't believe me. "Just one time?"

"Yeah," I said. "I think so."

I didn't like the look on Heather's face. Her eyes narrowed. The looks she'd been giving me just a few minutes earlier had felt so much better.

She went on, "Oh, come on, just this once can't *really* hurt him. We're asking you to stay, Nicki. And it's kind of fun to see him not act so perfect. It's kind of cute to see him go a little nuts, like a regular puppy."

But I knew that was exactly the problem. Sprocket had to learn to *not* behave like a regular dog. He could *not* go nuts. And after all the progress he'd made, it would confuse him. After all the discipline, he'd think *I'd* gone nuts.

Heather said, "You're one of us now, Nicki. Come on, can't you just stay? It won't hurt anything."

But it could. Time spent in another person's home was supposed to be for training only. But what else had Heather said? *You're one of us now, Nicki.*

I looked at Kris, who was focusing down on the

floor. I wished she would look up and say something, just agree with me about Sprocket. *Rescue me,* I thought. She wasn't pressuring me to stay like Heather was, but she wasn't exactly standing up for me, either.

Finally I kind of eked out, "Service dogs have to stay under the control of their owners. He's not supposed to go crazy like this."

Heather sighed, exasperated. Then she said, "I'm really disappointed in you, Nicki. I thought for a while there you were going to be fun. Come on, don't go."

I looked at her face. She seemed to be offering me something only if I stayed and let everyone have fun with Sprocket, something like an entrance into their world. Being friends with Heather and Kris and even Amanda and Marcy could gain me a whole different life at school. I had seen the way people watched them all the time, and I couldn't help being a little envious of the way they could get away with doing or saying anything and still be considered cool. That would sure make my life easier. It'd be nice having people admire you and want to hang around you all the time.

But I'd never cared very much about popularity; I'd always had Becca and other friends, too.

"Come on," said Heather again, impatiently.

I felt paralyzed for a moment. Could it really

hurt to let Sprocket play a little crazily just one time? If I said "No," then Heather would dislike me again. If I said "Yes," I'd be admitted into her circle.

I almost did it, just to keep from having to say that one little word. But then I looked down at Sprocket, and my eyes locked on his. He was looking up at me with that loving, trusting expression. He trusted me. Mom trusted me. Mrs. Tate trusted me to do this the right way. And I wanted to do it right, too.

But more than anything else, *Sprocket* had worked so hard to get it right. He had come this far. He had learned and trained and exercised his heart out. He had shown the makings of a good service dog; even I could see that. I couldn't set him back, I couldn't let him fail—even if it meant I would be giving him up someday. It wouldn't be fair to *him*. And that was more important than something like popularity.

And so I did the other thing, you know, that thing I could never do before: I put my tongue on the roof of my mouth behind my teeth and made a circle with my lips, and it came out stronger and surer than I thought it would, stronger and surer than I could've imagined myself sounding.

"No," I said.

A Big Word

"No."

11

Help

The world didn't come to an end.

Before I left, Heather acted as though she found me an annoyance again, and when Dad came to pick us up, she barely mumbled, "Bye."

On the way home Dad kept glancing over at me as if he was concerned or something, but I could only look straight ahead at the road, lined with new green grasses and early spring wildflowers.

The world hadn't exactly come to an end, but how could such pretty little yellow flowers be blooming when I felt this awful? Sprocket whimpered a bit from the back seat, as if he was feeling the same way, too.

"What's wrong?" Dad asked me.

"Nothing," I said.

He looked straight ahead, too. Finally he sighed, "Okay, but if you want to talk about it—"

"I don't," I said, asking him with my eyes to understand. It was a trick I'd learned from Sprocket.

"Okay."

At home I got out of the pickup truck and headed inside and toward my room, Sprocket at my side. Mom

called from the kitchen, where she was clearing the
table after making dinner. Obviously she'd had a good
day. "We tried to wait for you," she said. "But I made
you a plate. I'll heat it up in the microwave."

I said, "Thanks, but I'm not hungry," and kept
on walking.

"Wait," she said. "I have to talk to you anyway.
I have to ask you a favor. Do you have time to help
Adam with his math later? And the dishes—"

"NO!" I cut her off, too. "NO, NO, NO."

I turned and left. Now that I'd learned to say
"No," I found out that it wasn't that hard after all.

I went into my room and closed the door, taking
Sprocket with me. He was looking at me as if he wanted
to connect with me, but not with a simple yes or no
question. He just wanted to talk with his eyes and his
face. It was just him and me now, and it felt as if we
were fighting the whole world.

Outside I heard Dad telling Mom and Adam to
leave me alone for a while. At least Dad understood.
Maybe that's why he spent so much time outside with
the animals. They couldn't ask you for something every
minute of the day.

Sprocket was still looking at me. I got down on
the floor and petted his head and scratched behind his

ears. His tongue was hanging out, and he gave me one of his great big grins. My eyes started to burn. But I told myself, *Don't cry. Nicki Fleming is the reliable one; she doesn't fall apart.*

A little later, Mom came to the door and brought me dinner, along with some cookies she'd baked earlier. "Here you go. I'm off to bed now." She pointed to her ankles—swollen again. "Dad is doing the dishes." She waited for a minute. "Nicki, look at me. I'm here to help, if you need me."

I took the plate and nodded, but I knew if I said anything, I would lose it and cry.

After that, Adam brought me a painting he had done at art class in school. Again, I just took it and barely managed a tiny "Thank you."

When Becca called, I decided to answer. She was probably going to be giving me a hard time. So what? What was one more thing?

"I'm surprised you're at home," she started, and a stone sank in my stomach. "I thought you'd be with your new friends."

"They aren't friends."

"No?"

"NO, not even close," I said. "Especially not Heather."

"What happened?"

I sighed. "I don't want to talk about it right now."

"Come on, please. Tell me."

"No, not right now." Then I eased up. Becca was worried, and I could tell. "I'll tell you the next time we see each other in person, but not on the bus. Okay?"

She said, "Okay."

After a few seconds of silence, Becca said, "So you don't have two new best friends?"

"No way."

She waited for a few minutes. "I have something to tell you. Being around Emily is fun, but not the same. Do you know what I mean?"

"Yeah," I said, and smiled. "I know exactly what you mean."

At least one thing was back to normal, sort of.

At school the next day, Heather wouldn't look at me. Heather, Kris, and I handed out our lists of teams and assignments for the gala, but we hardly talked to one another. Becca and I ate lunch together as usual, and after school, Mrs. Baxter asked Heather, Kris, and me to stay behind for a minute.

"I want to congratulate you," she said. "The three of you did a beautiful job on the planning for the gala. I think it's going to be terrific. You came up with a unique and interesting theme."

We just stood there.

"Anything wrong?" she asked.

I think we all shook our heads at the same time. I gathered up my backpack and started to head out fast. I could still catch the bus and ride with Becca. But before I hit the front door of the school, Kris came running up behind me.

"Nicki—hold on," she said.

I stopped and turned around to face her.

"It wasn't nice what Heather did to you and Sprocket. Sometimes I don't know about her . . ."

I just waited.

"I should have stood up for you," she said. "You couldn't hurt your dog, and I get it." She sighed. "Anyway, I'm still hoping that you'll come over to my house sometime. Bring Sprocket, and I promise not to turn it into a party. You can meet my cat. Her name is Pumpkin, because she's kind of orange."

I smiled a tiny bit for the first time that day.

"So, will you still come over sometime?"

My first impulse was to say "No." Funny, now that I'd started to say it, it was kind of coming naturally to me. But Kris was looking at me as if she really wanted me to come, so finally I said, "Maybe. We'll see what happens."

"Okay."

That night before bedtime, I took Sprocket out for his last walk of the day. Mom had said that I could

start letting him off the leash for short periods of play-
time, and something told me he needed this; he needed
a few moments of freedom. I let him loose and then sat
down under the rear porch lights and pulled out my
sketch pad. I looked at a watercolor I'd done of Jackson
and the last sketch I'd done of Sprocket and the butterfly. When I looked up again, Sprocket was gone.

I stood up, searching for him. A moment later
I heard whimpering. Out of the darkness Sprocket came
back into view. At first I couldn't see what was wrong.
Then, in the light, I saw two porcupine quills sticking
out of his nose like darts. Ugh. I should've thought of
that. This was the time of night when all of the wildlife
was out, and Sprocket had let his curiosity get the
better of him. Or more likely, a porcupine had gotten
the better of him. Sprocket was whimpering and panting and looking to me for help. He was hurting, bad.

I got Dad. We took Sprocket into the barn, where
Dad said he had to be the one to hold Sprocket down,
because I wasn't strong enough. But that left me to be
the one to pull out the quills with needle-nose pliers.
Sprocket yelped when I grabbed the first quill and
gently pulled, like Dad told me to. Two big drops
of blood oozed out behind the quills. Sprocket whined
loudly, like a cry, when I pulled out the next one. It

felt as though I had just punctured my own skin.

"There, there," I said and tried not to cry. Dad just said, "He's going to be all right, Nicki. You did that very well."

Afterward, Dad and I cleaned Sprocket's wounds and applied some medicated ointment, and then I took Sprocket inside and stayed with him for a long time until he was calm again. "I'm sorry, Sprocket," I said over and over. "I won't let that happen again."

With my journal open in front of me, I held the pen and thought about what to write about Sprocket. I felt bad about the porcupine quills, but otherwise Sprocket was doing great, and he felt like he was mine. So what more was there to say, except . . .

I love him.

12

Gala

I took Sprocket to the gala, his first big outing at which he'd have to deal with a large group of people. Mrs. Tate had said she thought it would be okay, because Sprocket was doing so well and Mom would be there to help me. And even though there would be noise and music, it wasn't the sort of thing that would get out of control. We all thought he was ready.

As soon as I led him out of the pickup, he listened to my commands and walked at my side. He didn't sniff or lick anyone, and even his tail was still.

We sat with Adam and my parents and with Becca and her parents. Sprocket was settled at my feet, and Becca was at my side.

Becca and Sprocket were buds now. Becca and I had been talking about hiking up in the mountains as soon as we could and taking Sprocket with us. He'd have to learn to control himself with the smell of wild animals all around. But Sprocket could do it—I knew it. I couldn't believe that school was actually over and summer was here.

Gala

The choir sang, and the play was funny—a little too silly, in fact—but good.

Everyone commented on our decorations. When the lights went down, the plastic glow-in-the-dark stars glimmered on the ceiling. The team that had done the ceiling had even managed to shine a spotlight on the full, bone-white paper moon that hung there.

On the dark walls, the meadow scenes were rich with summer grasses, flowers, and animals. Someone had even put a few nighthawks hunting over the horizon. And the aluminum-foil stream in front of the stage looked just as Kris had said it would—like water lit up by the full moon.

Mrs. Baxter congratulated us in front of everyone. She said ours were the best gala decorations ever. And then all the parents and guests clapped. People kept saying that the night look was the best they had ever seen.

I couldn't believe we had actually done it.

I also couldn't believe that Kris was sitting by herself, or at least with only her parents. Heather stuck to Amanda and Marcy and some of the other new kids. She never even looked my way.

After it was over, Kris came up to Becca and me.

"Hi," she said.

We said "Hi" back. And then I didn't know what to say. I kind of felt sorry for her.

I didn't know if Becca would like the idea, but I asked Kris to come hiking with us sometime over the summer. Becca nodded her head in agreement. "Call me," I told Kris, "or I'll call you."

She broke into a big smile.

Before we left, some boys from my class, Jason and Matthew, came up to Sprocket and wanted to pet him, but I knew it might be too much. He'd had a big night and had handled it really well so far.

I said, "Not now. I know he's irresistible and all, but sometimes a handler has to say 'No.' Thanks for asking, though."

"Okay," Jason said and shrugged. "That's cool."

Instead they just looked at him and talked for a while. "How could I get into training a dog like this?" Matthew asked.

"I can give you the name of a lady to talk to. And there's a Web site with information, too."

"Thanks," Matthew said. He wasn't even mad about not petting Sprocket. I'd done it again—I could say "No," and it was okay.

When I looked down at Sprocket, he was giving me his classic big happy grin. I could tell he wanted a treat as a reward for his good behavior. After all, he had just passed a huge test—he'd behaved the way a service dog in training is supposed to, even sur-rounded by lots of people and noise and activity.

When I looked at Mom and Dad, Mom gave me the thumbs-up sign and Dad gave me a wink.

So I pulled out a special doggie pig-in-a-blanket from the bag, and Sprocket started wiggling, but only a little bit. "No. Wait," I said.

He held still before I gave him the snack.

"Good dog," I said.

And then his eyes said it all right back to me—*Good trainer.*

True Story

Meet two sisters in Colorado who, like Nicki, are puppy raisers. Each of them is putting her whole heart, mind, and energies into helping prepare their puppy for advanced training as a service dog.

When it comes to raising puppies, sisters 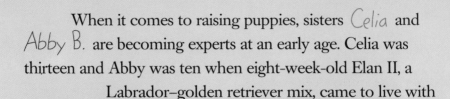 Celia and Abby B. are becoming experts at an early age. Celia was thirteen and Abby was ten when eight-week-old Elan II, a Labrador–golden retriever mix, came to live with them. Since his arrival, they have been busy raising Elan *(EE-lahn)* with their mother, Sandy. Like Nicki and her mom in the story, Celia, Abby, and Sandy are raising Elan to become a service or assistance dog that will help someone with physical disabilities live a more independent life.

Imagine not being able to open a door, turn on a light switch, or pick up something that you've dropped. Service dogs help people by doing all of those things—even tugging off clothing. They can pull wheelchairs, too. Some dogs are specially trained to be "hearing dogs" who alert someone who is deaf to important sounds, such as a baby's cry, a doorbell, or an alarm clock. Other service dogs' main role is to provide loving companionship to people with special needs.

Celia was the first in her family to hold Elan and welcome him!

A happy recipient of a service dog

When Celia and Abby's mother brought up the idea of raising and training a service dog, the girls were immediately interested. At that time, they didn't know anyone who had an assistance dog, but they both liked the idea that their efforts would eventually help someone with special needs live more independently—and, Celia says, "We thought it would be fun to have a new puppy in the house!"

*Puppies waiting
for their volunteer raisers*

How do you become a puppy raiser? Some puppies, like Nicki's dog, Sprocket, are "rescue" or "shelter" dogs—they are rescued from animal shelters and tested to see if they have the potential to become an assistance dog. But Elan came to Celia and Abby's family from Canine Companions for Independence (CCI), a program that not only trains dogs but also has a breeding program aimed at producing dogs with just the right temperament to become working dogs.

Sandy and the girls filled out an application and were interviewed by CCI volunteers. The final step was an in-home inspection, to be sure that their home was a safe environment for raising and training a puppy.

Once cleared for puppy raising, Sandy, Celia, and Abby waited eagerly for their puppy to arrive. Celia was to be the official co-raiser with Sandy, while Abby planned to reinforce more than actually teach the many commands a service dog must learn.

Elan and another pup arrive with their "flight angel"—Tom, an airline employee who flies pups to puppy raisers around the country when he is off-duty. The puppies travel in soft-sided carriers that fit under the airplane seats.

When Elan finally arrived, the whole family immediately fell in love with him—even Celia and Abby's dad, Matt, who initially wasn't as involved as the rest of the family in the puppy raising. Now, however, Elan regularly accompanies Matt to work!

Elan is on a special outing with another service dog. Both dogs are learning to behave well in public.

Right from the start, Elan was treated differently from their pet dog. "I had to get used to not being able to play just any old way with Elan," says Abby. "No rough play with people is allowed, because that can encourage aggression and the urge to dominate." Games like tug-of-war are also discouraged because service dogs need to learn that pulling is for opening cabinets or refrigerator doors, not for play.

In addition to commands such as "Sit," "Stay," and "Down," Abby and Celia are also gently teaching Elan not to be possessive of his toys and food. "Elan is being taught to serve others, not to be served," says Celia.

Abby and Elan enjoy playing during some downtime.

The girls say that Elan's training involves gentle firmness, consistency, repetition, and lots of loving reinforcement. In addition to learning commands, service

dogs are gradually exposed to a wide variety
of people and settings so that they can learn
socialization skills and not to be fearful, no matter
where they are. As Elan has gotten older, he
has gone almost everywhere the family
goes—to the recreation center, to Matt's
office, to the library, and even shopping.
But Elan rarely goes to school. "It's too
much for the *kids*," laughs Celia.

Elan's service-dog cape lets people know that he is a working dog.

Celia and Abby's family will
turn Elan in for advanced training after
about eighteen months. Saying good-bye to the dog that has
become part of their family will be very difficult, but knowing
that Elan has an important job to do helps prepare them for

Abby, Celia, and Elan

that difficult day. Celia says, "He's going
to do something great for someone, and
that makes me proud. You have to be
willing to let the dog go."

If Elan is not successful in
advanced training, Celia and Abby's
family will have the option to adopt
him as a pet. But if he does well with
advanced training, they'll get to attend
his graduation and meet his partner—the
person he'll be paired with. "When that
happens, I'll be both sad *and* proud,"
says Abby.

Raising Canines

Visit these Web sites to find out about what it takes to become a puppy raiser or a service-dog trainer or about other ways to help those who are raising assistance dogs:

You can learn more about Canine Companions for Independence, the organization that Celia and Abby's family is working with, by visiting their Web site at **www.cci.org**.

Find out about one of the programs that works specifically with shelter dogs by visiting **www.freedomservicedogs.org**.

There are programs and organizations that provide assistance dogs in just about every state. Visit **www.wags.net** to see what the Wisconsin Academy of Graduate Service Dogs (WAGS) is up to.

Assistance-Dog Etiquette

Here are some tips about assistance-dog etiquette that will help you when you meet a person with a service dog. It's important to remember that the dog is working, and you should not do anything to iv the dog from performing its tasks.

- **Do** speak to the person first.
- **Do** just ignore the dog.
- **Do** keep in mind that the dog has a very important job to do.
- **Do** be aware that assistance dogs are allowed in public places.
- **Do** know that the dog loves to work and is well treated.
- **Do** remember that the dog is friendly and lovable.
- **Do** teach others that the dog is working.

- **Don't** talk to, call, or make sounds at the dog.
- **Don't** touch the assistance dog without asking permission.
- **Don't** let others freely pet the dog.
- **Don't** feed the assistance dog.
- **Don't** give commands to the dog; this is the owner's job.
- **Don't** ask personal questions about the handler's disability or intrude on his or her privacy.
- **Don't** be offended if the handler declines to chat about the assistance dog.
- **Don't** be offended if you are asked not to pet the dog.

Meet the Author

Ann Howard Creel lives outside Denver, Colorado. In addition to being an author, she is a school nurse. Her first books with American Girl were *A Ceiling of Stars* and *Nowhere Now Here,* a book about alpaca farmers. She has three sons and a dog and a cat and loves the mountains as much as Nicki does.

Meet the Real Sprocket

When author Ann Creel started to write a story about a girl who helps raise a service dog, she turned to her friend Jessica, who had done just that. Ann fell in love with the dog that Jessica helped raise and named Nicki's fictional dog "Sprocket" in his honor. The real Sprocket is a golden retriever Jessica sometimes calls "Sprocket the Rocket" because of his high energy level! When Sprocket wasn't able to complete advanced training, Jessica and her husband adopted him as their pet.